"Do You Know What You've Been Up To, Bucko?"

The face mask was ripped away, the furious action followed by the huffy question, "Who's asking?"

Paul could only stare. His mouth dropped open, but any words he might have spoken froze in his mouth. Everything in body and mind froze along with his verbal skills.

He was staring down into a pair of big brown eyes that looked as soft and beautiful as a fawn's, even with the added sparkle of temper. More shocking yet, they shone from the oval face of a Madonna. High cheekbones, small chin, delicate nose, magnolia skin and the sweetest mouth he'd ever seen. Angelic features combined to perfection and framed by shimmering waves of silky black hair.

It was her!

Dear Reader,

Welcome to Silhouette! Our goal is to give you hours of unbeatable reading pleasure, and we hope you'll enjoy each month's six new Silhouette Desires. These sensual, provocative love stories are both believable and compelling—sometimes they're poignant, sometimes humorous, but always enjoyable.

Indulge yourself. Experience all the passion and excitement of falling in love along with our heroine as she meets the irresistible man of her dreams and together they overcome all obstacles in the path to a happy ending.

If this is your first Desire, I hope it'll be the first of many. If you're already a Silhouette Desire reader, thanks for your support! Look for some of your favorite authors in the coming months: Stephanie James, Diana Palmer, Dixie Browning, Ann Major and Doreen Owens Malek, to name just a few.

Happy reading!

Isabel Swift
Senior Editor

SDRL-7/85

JOYCE THIES
False Pretenses

Silhouette Desire

Published by Silhouette Books New York

America's Publisher of Contemporary Romance

SILHOUETTE BOOKS
300 East 42nd St., New York, N.Y. 10017

Copyright © 1987 by Joyce Thies

ISBN: 0-373-05359-2

First Silhouette Books printing June 1987

America's Publisher of Contemporary Romance

Printed in the U.S.A.

Books by Joyce Thies

Silhouette Desire

Territorial Rights #147
Spellbound #348
False Pretenses #359

*written as Melissa Scott

JOYCE THIES

has authored or coauthored over twenty contemporary and historical novels. Readers might recognize her as the Joyce half of Janet Joyce. She wrote her first Silhouette Desire, *Territorial Rights*, as Melissa Scott, but is now writing under her own name.

Joyce didn't realize how much pig lore existed until she began her research for *False Pretenses*. It was a bit humbling for her to find out that hogs have been rooting about the earth for at least forty-five million years, whereas man can only claim a million. Perhaps it is this awesome eternalness that has evoked such hogrophobia in man. In Scotland, for example, traditional belief held that just saying the word "pig" could bring on a natural disaster.

On the other hand, this much maligned creature has inspired some eloquent poetical reflection by some of the world's most distinguished authors. To her chagrin, Joyce discovered that two such works, *Quo Vadis Porcus?* and *The Mighty Anglo-Saxon Hog Uprising*, went right over her head. However, she did find *Hogs in Love: A Study in Sensitivity* very worthwhile and informative.

Prologue

Paul Lansing didn't like surprises. As a special agent for the FBI, he made it his business to avoid them. Nevertheless, Sam Mitchell, unit chief of the Chicago bureau, often managed to catch him unawares—which annoyed Paul and amused Sam no end. When it came to keeping his men on their toes, the plump, balding, middle-aged gnome had no equal.

As Paul repeated dumbly, "You want me to hire myself out to a pig farm in Podunk, Iowa?" his self-complacent superior didn't even bother to stifle his elfin chuckle.

"That's what I said," Mitchell confirmed, lacing his pudgy fingers behind his gleaming head as he leaned back in his desk chair. "As soon as this assignment came down, I knew you were the right man for the job."

Having worked under Sam Mitchell for almost fifteen years, Paul knew he didn't stand a chance of outlasting him when it came to a battle of wills. In this mischievous mood, the chief wouldn't divulge one more detail until it was asked for, and the longer an agent delayed asking, the more Mitchell enjoyed himself at said agent's expense.

With a long-suffering sigh, Paul gave in and took the bait. "Okay, you ornery old buzzard, I'll bite. Why me?"

"Didn't you announce to me just a few days ago that you want to retire early and become a farmer?"

Paul felt a sinking sensation in the pit of his stomach as he pondered the implications. The more he thought about Mitchell's motives for asking, the more wary and suspicious he became. "If I did, I certainly didn't intend for the information to become part of the public record."

"But that *is* what you said?"

Remembering how drunk he'd been on the occasion of his thirty-eighth birthday, Paul knew it was entirely possible. Considering how much else he might have revealed about himself that night and had since forgotten, Paul's wintry gray eyes frosted over even more. When he spoke again, his tone no longer held any deference for a greater authority. "I thought that conversation was strictly between us, Sam. You knew I was blitzed."

When the older man gave him what could only be described as an affectionately paternal nod, Paul groaned, "Don't bother giving me that 'it's all in the family' stuff. I get the picture."

He gestured angrily toward the closed door that separated them from the other agents assigned to the office. "When I walk out this door I can expect any one of those turkeys to spout off on this subject, can't I? Thanks a whole lot, Chief. That's just what I needed right now."

"What you need is a chance to find out if you're doing the right thing, Lancelot," Mitchell stated, emphasizing the nickname Paul had been given as a rookie. Like the courageous knights of old, he'd charged right in where even angels feared to tread. Over the following fifteen years, Paul hadn't changed and the nickname had stuck.

"Let me remind you that retirement from the force lasts forever," Mitchell continued, highly irritated when the comment brought no more than a dismissing lift of one dark brow. "Dammit, Lansing! If you choose to trade your white charger for a plow horse, the only kind of dragons you'll be slaying in the future are the kind that don't stay dead. Bad weather, crop failure, unending financial woes. Year after year, you'll fight the same frustrating battles and work harder than you've ever worked in your life just to keep your head above water. Is that what you want to do with the rest of your life?"

Paul went rigid at the question. He'd posed it to himself over and over again in the past few weeks and still didn't have an answer. He hated not having an answer and that made him all the more defensive. "Since when did a street kid from the Bronx become such an expert on farming?"

"Since my top agent told me he's considering laying down his gun to pick up a hoe," Mitchell retorted just as sarcastically. "It makes no sense and we both know it. If you think you're going to recapture your lost youth down on the farm, you're kidding yourself. You ran away from that life once before. What makes you think you won't do it again?"

The only thing that kept Paul in his chair was his many years of training in the art of staying calm under fire. "Exactly how much did I tell you the other night, Chief Mitchell?"

The chief's implacable blue eyes met his agent's intense gray ones head on and never wavered. "Your folks are dead, Agent Lansing. You can't prove anything to them by throwing away your career and taking up their way of life without giving it a hell of a lot more thought. When you do make the decision to go or to stay, it's got to be for yourself, not because you think you owe your father something. Whatever you decide, he's not going to know or care."

For the first time in their association, Paul felt like slamming his fist into Sam Mitchell's face and Sam knew it. Sam even thought he deserved it, but that didn't stop him from using any weapon he had at his disposal to keep one of his most highly skilled agents from resigning prematurely. "Take this assignment, Lansing. If you do, you'll not only be performing a great service for your country, but you just might find the answers to all those difficult questions you've been asking yourself ever since you flew down to West Virginia to bury your folks."

Through clenched teeth, Paul challenged, "And if I don't do my patriotic duty?"

Mitchell fired the last shot contained in his meager arsenal. "'Then you'll lose the only chance you'll ever get to nail the 'Scarlet Lady.'"

One

On a cold night in February, the city streets of Chicago were streaked with brown slush and lined with banks of dirty snow. A never-ending flow of traffic, whizzing trains and bustling crowds provided a constant noise. Bright lights shone from all directions—headlights, streetlights, flashing safety signals, lighted skyscrapers. Lights everywhere.

On a cold night in February, the back roads of Iowa were slick with ice and lined with overwhelming mountains of stark, white snow. There was no traffic, no people and no noise. Occasionally, a flickering beacon indicated the location of a distant farmhouse, then faded quickly out of sight.

Pinpoints of stars shone in the fathomless heavens. A chilling white moon cast a crystalline gleam over the vast fields of undisturbed snow, but the sky still seemed dark, a magnificent black canopy stretching out to infinity. As he drove slowly along the desolate highway, the wheels of his pickup crunching on the packed snow, Paul was struck by an overwhelming sense of isolation.

Known as a loner and liking it that way, he was amazed at his unease, discomfited by the tiny prickles he felt rising on the back of his neck. Because of his job, he was surrounded by the nefarious activities of murderers and thieves, yet he'd never experienced the kind of uncertainty he was feeling now. Out in the middle of nowhere with nothing and nobody to fear, why should he be anxious?

The answer was a self-revelation, the truth of it bringing a wry grin. He'd been alone often, but not this alone since childhood. On the other side of his apartment walls, his office door, his car window, he was always surrounded by the presence of others. Here, the only human presence he felt was his own and outside the window, the mighty hand of nature was closing in. Compared to his surroundings, he felt pretty damned insignificant.

"Macho, macho man," he sang loudly into the bitterly cold, black night, taking great comfort in the sound of his own voice. "I wanna be a macho man."

Five miles farther down the road, his voice trailed away as he braked to a stop, then reached for the map lying next to him on the seat. "This has to be it," he decided, comparing the right-hand turnoff with the tiny black line on the map. "Rural Route 16."

Staring through the windshield, he sighted a tiny, incandescent glow that told him that his exhausting, ten-hour drive from Chicago was nearly over. If he'd found the right road, that light had to be coming from his destination. As he made the turn and continued

driving, he surveyed the hilly, snow-covered land-
scape on either side of the narrow road.

His headlights glanced off groves of oak, maple and
spruce, their branches decked out in glistening snow.
He saw quaint wooden fences crisscrossing the de-
serted fields, an ancient windmill marking time and
finally the hand-painted metal mailbox bearing the
name he sought. Heading down the long, slated
driveway, he viewed a three-story white house with
gingerbread trim, a large white barn and several
wooden outbuildings nestled cozily together at the
bottom of the hill. It was hard to believe such a pic-
turesque, Currier-and-Ives setting could house an
abomination to mankind, but the evidence couldn't be
denied.

In all probability, this was the home of the "Scarlet
Lady," the notorious Mafia hit woman who commanded a top spot on the FBI's list of most wanted
criminals, her unknown identity notwithstanding.

Without even realizing it, Paul brought the truck to
a complete stop to take a long, hard look at the place.
Before starting up again, he heard an odd noise and
rolled down his window to identify it. The muffled
roar increased in volume the closer it came. And it was
getting close, very close.

Paul blinked at the sight that greeted him next, a
sight that in no way matched the sound he was hearing. Dogs! A pack of dogs surged up out of the ditch
onto the drive, directly in front of his wheels. Obviously, they were far more terrified of whatever was
chasing them than they were of the headlights bearing
down on them from his truck. If he'd been moving, he
would've hit any number of them.

Tongues hanging out, lungs heaving, the dogs raced
across the drive and quickly disappeared into a stand
of fir trees on the opposite side. A second later, a
speeding snowmobile came up out of the same ditch
in hot pursuit of the dogs. Showing no more concern
for the presence of his truck than the dogs had demonstrated, the roaring machine zipped right in front of
him, jumped over the next ditch and careened off
across the deep snow.

In the instant before it, too, disappeared between
two spruce trees, Paul caught a glimpse of its menia-
cal driver. In his line of work, all he needed was a
glimpse to tell a lot. The operator was probably a
teenage boy. The kid had long legs, but the narrow
shoulders indicated he hadn't yet reached full matu-
rity. The crazy stunt he'd just pulled clinched that estimation.

He was dressed in a dark snowmobile suit and
heavy, black boots that laced up over the ankle. His
driving gloves sported orange glow-in-the-dark stripes.
On his head was a black, fiberglass helmet with a clear
visor. Beneath the visor, he wore an orange, woolen
face mask that made it impossible to identify his features.

Making another kind of identification had been
easy. Paul had recognized the make and model of the
high-powered rifle slung over the driver's shoulder as
soon as he'd seen it. Fired at long range, it could still
put a very large hole in a dog, or for that matter, a
man. Whoever had placed such a high-caliber weapon
in the hands of a boy had to have a few screws loose.

Paul had a good idea who that person might be, but
he wasn't sure about the boy. According to his
sources, there were only two people residing at the

farm—the female suspect and her eighty-year-old grandmother.

He hadn't been informed of any teenager, but that didn't mean company hadn't arrived since the surveillance team had left. Their last report had indicated that several relatives lived within the state and paid regular visits to the farm. He'd read that one or two of the great-nephews were teenage males. Since there weren't any neighbors for miles, the less than safety conscious kid on the snowmobile had to be a visiting relative and an unforeseen complication.

Keeping a wary eye open for the reappearance of either the dogs or the armed adolescent on their trail, Paul eased the pickup into a forward gear and proceeded slowly to the end of the drive. He parked the truck in the brightest glow of the yard light, but he didn't get out. His plans didn't include getting himself shot, not even accidentally, so he waited.

Paul heard the snowmobile returning before he saw it. By the time it pulled up in front of the barn and the driver shut off the engine, Paul had gotten out of the truck and was striding toward him. When the kid turned round, Paul was there, his anger evident. "I hope you realize what almost happened out there, buddy. You're very lucky my truck wasn't moving!"

A gloved hand lifted the helmet's visor and a defiant voice spoke from behind the orange face mask. "I saw you."

"At the speed you were going, you couldn't see squat!" Paul declared, dismissing the claim with a sarcastic snort. "That's not a popgun you're carrying. If you'd bounced the wrong way, it could've blown your head off. Bet you never thought of that, did you?"

"Didn't have to." With slow, deliberate movements the helmet was removed, then set down on the
seat of the snowmobile. "The safety catch was on."

"The reckless way you were driving, it could have
jarred loose. Didn't anybody ever teach you sense?
What kind of an idiot would go off by himself to chase
after a pack of wild dogs? Do your parents know what
you've been up to, bucko?"

The face mask was ripped away, the furious action
followed by the huffy question, "Who's asking?"

Paul could only stare. His mouth dropped open, but
any words he might have spoken froze in his mouth.
Everything in his body and his mind froze along with
his verbal skills.

He was staring down into a pair of big brown eyes
that looked as soft and beautiful as a fawn's, even with
the added sparkle of temper. More shocking yet, they
shone from the oval face of a Madonna, who had high
cheekbones, a small chin, a delicate nose, magnolia
skin and the sweetest mouth he'd ever seen. Angelic
features were combined to perfection and framed by
shimmering waves of silky, black hair.

It was her! Paul knew it was her, but for the life of
him, he couldn't reconcile this lovely, doe-eyed creature with the pictures he'd been shown of their suspect. Not one of them had done her justice. Not one
had warned him of what to expect when meeting her
in person. Her coloring was the only thing the woman
standing before him had in common with her pictures.

Sam Mitchell's voice came back to him. "Prime
suspect, Patricia Courteau, female Caucasian, age
thirty-two, hair black, eyes brown, no distinguishing
marks or features...."

Thousands of women filled that description, but not this one. She was one of a kind. That thought bolted through him like a charge of electricity and with it came a realization that wrenched all the oxygen out of his lungs. Any woman who accepted money to commit murder had to be unique. He'd known that about her all along. Why, then, was he so surprised, even shocked to discover what she actually looked like?

He couldn't accept the logical answer. Since he knew what she did for a living, there was no way he could want her. The sudden tightness in his groin had to be caused by something other than desire, especially since he'd personally viewed the stiffened remains of those men who'd foolishly allowed her to lure them into her bed. He'd sooner sleep with a black widow spider than with this woman. Beneath her angelic looks, beat the heart of a deadly viper.

Tricia tried very hard to stay calm under the man's fierce, penetrating gaze but it still sent shivers up her spine. Who the dickens was he and what possible business could he have here? The assessing way he was staring at her conjured up some pretty frightening possibilities.

As unobtrusively as possible, she lowered her shoulder, grasping hold of the butt of the rifle as it swung against her hip. Cradling the stock on her forearm, she rotated her arm and the leather strap slid silently over her elbow. Freed of the constriction, her hand inched toward the firing lock. With her finger coiled securely around the trigger, she felt much more confident about her ability to handle any false moves on his part.

Taking a deep breath, she brought up the rifle barrel to make sure he realized she was now in command of the weapon. He didn't need to know that she wasn't capable of shooting a fellow human being. Armed by false bravado, she challenged, "You didn't seem to have any trouble expressing yourself a few seconds ago, mister. What happened? Cat got your tongue?"

"You're . . . you're no kid."

Was that why he'd been so taken aback when she'd pulled off her helmet, Tricia asked herself as she stared up at him. For some reason, she thought not, sensing there was a deeper, far more dangerous meaning behind his halting statement. She was intimidated by the feeling, but even more so by the man who didn't seem the least bit nervous at having a gun pointed in his direction.

As males went, he was an impressive specimen. At five six, Tricia wasn't short, but he was a good six inches taller and breadthwise, he was twice her size. Though his features were in shadow, they appeared rugged, not quite handsome, yet supremely masculine. She searched his face for any sign of anger and found none.

"No, I'm not," she agreed after a moment, immediately wary again when he didn't say anything else, nor break off his perturbing appraisal. Since his back was to the light, she couldn't quite make out the color of his eyes, but they continued their slow inventory of her face, feature by feature. It wasn't a sensual accounting. Oddly enough, she would have felt safer if it was.

When his piercing gaze reached her chin, she lifted it and the barrel of her gun another notch higher. Stretching the truth only slightly, she disclosed, "I own this place and I want to know who you are and what you're doing here within five seconds. In case you're unaware of it, bucko, this is private property and you're trespassing.''

"Paul Lansing," he offered and held out his hand.

Did he actually think she was going to accept the friendly gesture from a man who, besides yelling his head off at her, had nearly scared her out of her wits? Snubbing the suspicious offer, Tricia took a step back, her gaze moving from his outstretched hand to his face. The smile that suddenly appeared there hit her with the devastating force of double-barreled dimples and flashing white teeth.

Recovering from the impact of that smile was a struggle, but somehow she managed. "Am I supposed to recognize the name?"

"I'm your new hired hand," he announced in what could only be described as a jovial tone.

"You're what!" Tricia demanded, totally dumfounded.

"Amos sent me," he said, as if giving the secret password that assured his immediate admittance into her good graces.

The only Amos in Tricia's acquaintance was their hired hand of thirty years, Amos Redding. As far as she knew, until his unexpected departure to Pennsylvania last week to see a brother they hadn't known existed, the gentle giant had never traveled more than fifty miles away from the farm in any direction. He couldn't possibly know a man like Paul Lansing, let alone have sent him as a replacement. "Amos?" she queried, sounding as if she'd never heard of the name.

"That's right. Amos Redding. I'm a friend of his brother, Jim."

"His brother, Jim," Tricia repeated, recognizing the name, but still leery of the man who mouthed it. If

James Redding was anything like his brother, he wouldn't know a man like Paul Lansing, either. She didn't know much about this long-lost brother, but did know that he lived in a place named Sawyer's Junction that called to mind a town of about the same size as nearby Quincy.

Lansing might be wearing faded jeans, a sheepskin-lined vest and a plaid flannel shirt, but he still had "Big City" written all over him. One glance at the expert razor cut of his dark brown hair and she could tell that. Beyond that, he wasn't wearing any gloves, and had shoes on instead of boots. If he had any idea of what it was like out in the country in below-zero weather, he'd have worn the proper gear.

Tricia realized that her next question was rife with suspicion and she didn't care. "Why should I believe you?"

"Why shouldn't you?" he countered reasonably.

"Because Amos wouldn't send somebody out here without telling us about it."

Paul shrugged. "If Amos didn't send me, how do I know that you're Patricia Courteau, not exactly the owner of the farm, but the owner's granddaughter?"

Reminded of her recent lie, Tricia was thoroughly annoyed by the knowledge that he'd seen right through it. "Which still gives me the right to question anyone who steps one foot on this property!"

Paul reared back and held out his hands palms up. "Hey! I'm sorry we got off to such a bad start. At the time, I didn't know who you were."

"You still don't," Tricia was compelled to remind him, though she had the oddest impression he knew far more than she would have liked. Had Amos spoken at length to him about her? She didn't like that idea at all. She had enough trouble dealing with her grandmother's constant matchmaking. She didn't need Amos working on her case, too.

"Not yet anyway," Paul agreed, determined to be pleasant. If she refused to let him in the door, he was in trouble. "If you want to know the truth, I thought you were some crazy kid who'd somehow gotten his hands on a gun and went off half-cocked."

He paused, his low, husky voice causing goose bumps to raise on her arms. "I was wrong."

"Very wrong," she said, the words coming out far more sharply than she'd intended. For some reason, she couldn't help feeling threatened by this man, even if his explanation for being here turned out to be the truth. Maybe it was the way he kept staring at her, as if he knew things about her he had no business knowing.

"You weren't exactly looking both ways when you crossed the driveway," he reproved softly, the slight note of male arrogance in his tone raising her feminist hackles. "You have to admit, it was a stupid thing to do."

"At this time of night, I wasn't expecting visitors," Tricia said, knowing it was a weak excuse. Being prepared for the unexpected was a prerequisite of snowmobiling at night and though she didn't plan on admitting it, it would've been far too late to swerve out of his path if his truck had been moving. Her entire attention had been focused on the dogs, all of her energy centered on getting off one good shot before they got out of range.

As the man said, she'd been damned lucky. In a weird sort of way, she supposed she owed him something. His sudden movement interrupted her thoughts and also made her smile. He was shuffling his weight from one foot to the other, tucking his hands under his armpits to escape the biting cold. The least she could do was offer to continue this conversation inside.

Making up her mind, she lowered her rifle and started walking toward the house. As expected, he fell into step beside her. By mutual agreement, they walked fast. "We've been plagued by that pack of strays all month," Tricia explained. "People drive out here from the city and dump their unwanted pets. In order to survive, they run together. You wouldn't believe how brazen they've gotten. Tonight they came all the way up to the farrowing barn. It was a good thing that I spotted them when I did. Otherwise, we could have lost some of our most valuable Chester White breeders."

"I understand," he tendered magnanimously, though to him, a pig was a pig. He wouldn't know the difference between a "valuable" Chester White and any other kid of porker. Hopefully, he wouldn't be required to tell the difference.

As they stepped inside the porch, Paul couldn't resist asking. "What were you going to do if you caught up to them, Annie Oakley? Ride sidesaddle and shoot from the hip?"

Tricia stamped the snow from her boots, picturing his face under the soles. "If the situation called for it, I could do just that," she informed him sweetly.

"I don't doubt it," he replied in a tone that brought up her head. In the bright overhead porch light, Tricia could see the distinctive color of his eyes. They were gray, a deep, gun-metal gray, hard as steel, and she was sure they were more lethal than the high-caliber weapon she carried.

He saw her nervous shiver and smiled in that astonishing way of his that could melt the coldest heart. "I can't wait to meet your grandmother."

"Who's that?" Aurie May Courteau demanded as they entered the room, squinting at Paul through her wire-rimmed glasses. With a quick, spry motion that belied her arthritic knees, she stood up from the rocking chair placed near the stove and advanced on the twosome standing just inside the kitchen door. "Kinda late to come callin' whoever you are. You get stuck out on the road, young fella? That's what happens when you try speedin' on these icy roads. Serves you right, if that's what you were doin'. Endin' up in the ditch is just what you get."

"He didn't get stuck, Grannie. He says Amos sent him to work for us," Tricia interjected before her grandmother really got wound up on the subject of speeders. "Did Amos make any mention of this before he went off to visit his brother?"

"That old man only talks when he has to," Aurie grumbled, digging in the pocket of her apron for a letter Tricia knew nothing about. "You'd be Paul Lansing, I gather? Don't look much like a hired hand to me."

"Sorry, ma'am, but that's who I am," Paul supplied, trying not to laugh. This crusty old woman came as much a surprise to him as her granddaughter. They both made an unforgettable first impression. Patricia Courteau might look like sugar, but she was potent spice on the inside. Aurie was all spit and vinegar, inside and out.

Paul much preferred the latter combination. With the older woman, he'd always know exactly where he stood. With the younger, he'd have to be very careful. "I'm glad I could come and help out until Amos gets back. From what I could see, you've got quite a big place here."

"More than two women can handle." Tricia supplied what he'd left unsaid in an acerbic tone, making it clear how she felt about that chauvinistic assumption even if it was true. "Is that what Amos told you?"

Paul smiled pleasantly. "All he said was to hightail it over here and help out since he couldn't see his way clear to leave Jim until he's back on his feet again."

"What's he down with?" Tricia asked. The answer didn't come from Paul but from her grandmother who was apparently very well informed.

"Amos wrote that it's his sciatica," she said, shaking her head sympathetically. "My mother suffered with it off and on all her life. Nothin' to fool with, that's for sure. I recall one time she was laid up near three months."

"Three months!" Tricia exclaimed, horrified. "Amos could be gone that long?"

Paul shrugged his broad shoulders, then bestowed a warm glance on Aurie. "Ma'am, if you'll just tell me where I'm to sleep, I'll be up and at 'em first thing in the morning."

"A tad cocky, aren't cha?" Aurie said, and Tricia stifled a groan, recognizing the speculative gleam that came into her grandmother's eyes as she took stock of Lansing's well-muscled body.

As Tricia feared, Aurie was thinking that Amos had indeed sent them a live one, just as he'd promised in his letter. Knowing how few and far between handsome bachelors were in these parts, she decided it was

Tricia's lucky day. "And you're strong by the looks of it. I guess we could do worse."

Paul accepted the backhanded compliment graciously, demonstrating the charm that had had so little effect on the elderly woman's granddaughter. He flashed Aurie a broad smile, ignoring the disdainful look cast his way by a pair of big, brown eyes. "I'm sure that between the three of us, we'll manage just fine."

"Well, don't just stand there, boy," Aurie declared, beaming. "Bring in those dashing dimples and set yourself down here at the table where I can get a better look at 'em. Tricia, get this man a hot cup of coffee. He sure looks like he could use one."

Two

Lying in bed in her own room, Tricia heard the door at the end of the hall click shut. A few moments later, the creaking bedsprings told her that Paul Lansing had finally been released from the kitchen and had come upstairs to bed. She still couldn't believe that her grandmother had invited a perfect stranger into the house. The man had turned up out of nowhere in the middle of the night and no matter what he professed, he didn't look like any hired man she'd ever seen.

Con man was more like it. How else could he have charmed his way right past Grannie's defenses? Accomplishing that feat was no easy task. Aurie Courteau was known for having a very suspicious mind where outsiders were concerned. She couldn't abide strangers, especially males, and woe to any traveling salesman who stopped in at the farm. If Grannie's waspish tongue didn't chase them away, she brought out the broom.

Why, then, had Paul Lansing passed muster so effortlessly? As if she didn't know. Tricia flushed as she recalled the words Grannie had used to explain why her granddaughter had recently left her job with the airlines and come back to live on the farm. An explanation that before tonight, she'd thought amusing. "Poor, dear girl plans to start up her own business. She never married, you know."

To his credit, though it had been very clear what Grannie had hoped to achieve by imparting that information, Lansing had glossed over the awkward moment by asking Tricia about her future career plans. Reluctant to take part in any further conversation with the man, she'd still been glad to give him a brief rundown of her idea for marketing the various homemade wares that could be found in the area. To her surprise, he'd appeared genuinely interested in her ideas and had asked quite a few pertinent questions that she'd answered a bit desperately before pointing out the lateness of the hour.

Expecting him to be offered Amos's quarters over the garage, she'd been taken aback when Grannie had asked her to prepare a room for him. She would've liked to have argued over the wisdom of letting him sleep in the house, but with one look at Grannie's face, she knew she'd have lost. When Grannie's sharp, French-Canadian mind was made up, that was that.

Tricia had felt far less welcoming toward him and the man knew it. As she'd stood reluctantly from the table and stepped past him to mount the stairs, her feelings had been written plainly on her face. The

smug expression on his had been just as easy to read.
Score one for him.

From the laughter she'd heard drifting up the stairs
for the next hour, Tricia had no doubt that he'd scored
considerably more points in her absence, at least with
the resident matchmaker. Well, Grannie might be impressed by the man's roguish good looks and questionable charm, but she was not. Before taking him to
her bosom, she'd require a lot more information about
him.

Taking him to my bosom? Why on earth had she
chosen that figure of speech? She'd rather take a viper to her bosom than that hateful man. Just because
Grannie viewed him as prospective husband material
didn't mean that she was going to also, that was for
sure. Besides showing up under questionable circumstances, he was conceited and far too high-handed for
her tastes. She'd had enough dealings with that ob-
noxious type as a flight attendant, one more aspect of
her old job that she was definitely not going to miss.

After tomorrow, she doubted Grannie would have
much regard for the man either. Around here, the
work day started at 6:00 a.m., which was now only
four hours away. Tricia wondered just how ''up and
at 'em'' their temporary hired hand would be at that
hour in the morning. When Grannie rousted him out
of bed for breakfast, it wouldn't even be light outside.

''Early to bed and early to rise makes a man healthy,
wealthy and wise,'' Tricia recited Ben Franklin's motto
that her family had always taken to heart and fell
asleep with a beatific smile on her face, forgetting that
she would get no more sleep than the man down the
hall.

But the man down the hall wasn't sleeping. Though exhausted both physically and mentally, Paul was still wide awake. Naked beneath the thick layers of colorful patchwork quilts, he stared thoughtfully up at the pink flowered wallpaper that covered the bedroom's cove ceiling.

Moonlight filtered through the sheer white curtains on the windows. If he wanted to, he could make a thorough study of every object in the room without turning on a lamp, but he didn't want to. He'd seen and heard enough for one night. And, with the exception of her familiarity with a gun, none of it augmented the department's theory that Patricia Courteau and the "Scarlet Lady" were one in the same person.

Before meeting her, he'd felt sure they were on the right trail and he'd relished the opportunity of changing the circumstantial evidence they had against her into irrefutable proof. The two days he'd spent grilling Amos Redding had only enhanced his belief that the lady had something to hide. When it came to Patricia Courteau, Amos had been about as forthcoming as a clam, claiming over and over again that the department was barking up the wrong tree, but unable or unwilling to offer a single corroborating fact to back up that claim.

When first contacted by the bureau, Amos had stressed that his loyalty was to the Courteaus. The only way they'd been able to gain any cooperation from the man was by appealing to his sense of patriotic duty. Reluctantly, he'd agreed to comply with the fictitious story they'd concocted about his having a long, lost brother in order for Paul to take his place at the farm,

but he'd made it very clear, he was only doing so to
help clear Patricia's name.

It was Aurie Courteau who'd planted the first seeds
of doubt in Paul's mind concerning Patricia's guilt.
He'd spent the last hour listening to her give a detailed testimonial of her granddaughter's virtues from
earliest childhood on. If one believed the older woman's noticeably prejudiced, yet sincere opinion, Patricia was a sweet, affectionate child who'd matured into
a warm, loving woman. According to Aurie, Tricia's
recent arrival at the farm was a prime example of her
caring nature.

Several years back, Aurie's son, Mack and his wife,
Leona, had decided that the income from farming was
too unstable. They'd moved to Dubuque where Mack
had secured a steady job with a boiler company. Two
months ago, they'd called Tricia in Minneapolis and
informed her that Aurie was crippled up by a severe
bout of arthritis and that they thought it time for her
to sell out, too. They'd proposed to finance the place-
ment for Aurie in a retirement home where she could
live out her last years in comfort.

Patricia had offered a better solution for all concerned. Knowing it would take dynamite to remove
Aurie from the only home she'd ever known, Patricia
had given up her own career and returned to the family farm to look after her grandmother in her old age.

It was Aurie's opinion that Patricia had initially
conceived her plan for a country craft business in order to convince Aurie that she wasn't acting out of
pity. In theory, it would be a practical and economic
way of solving both their problems. Whenever Aurie
became too crippled by her recurring attacks of arthritis to move, Patricia would be there to make sure

all the work round the farm got done. In return, while Patricia found out if her business would be a success, Aurie would provide her with free room and board.

If Paul accepted that explanation as the truth, and Aurie had done all in her power to convince him that it was, Patricia was innocent and he'd been sent here on a wild-goose chase. Of course, it was still possible that the woman was a bad seed and an extraordinary actress. If all who knew her loved her, as the grandmother suggested, Patricia had been performing all her life. Sweet, warm, loving—none of those terms could be attributed to a cold-blooded killer like the "Scarlet Lady," unless she was even more diabolical than even he had imagined.

Or maybe she had a split personality. The odds didn't favor that theory, but Paul preferred that possibility to any other one he could think of. If he found out that the beautiful woman he'd just met was guilty, he'd just as soon find out that insanity was the underlying cause of her crimes. Considering the "Scarlet Lady's" modus operandi, that could well be true.

After luring her victim into bed, she injected them with a fast-acting, lethal drug when they were in the throes of passion. The only clue she left behind was her trademark—a bright, scarlet imprint of her lips on the victim's body. All twenty of the innocent and not so innocent men who'd died at her hands had literally been given the kiss of death.

The drug could be found in any veterinary practice and the brand of lipstick was one that could be bought at any cosmetic counter across the country. No fingerprints, blood, clothing or any other shred of evidence had ever been found at the scene. There was never the slightest sign of a struggle, which didn't help

Patricia's case any. If a woman who looked like her came to his bed, Paul wouldn't have put up much of a fight either.

"Knock it off, Lansing," Paul ordered under his breath, as a very erotic image sprang into his head. He dispelled the sudden ache in his loins by replacing Patricia's lovely face with the monstrous visage he'd imagined of the "Scarlet Lady." In the five years he'd been after her, he'd often pictured her like that, wanting to think she wasn't human. If she was, why hadn't she been subject to the same failings as those who worked so diligently toward her capture?

Because of her unbelievable success rate, the bureau had nothing to hang on the Mangioni family. Because of her, their criminal operations were flourishing. Because of her, he'd soon be slopping pigs.

"You asked for this, remember?" he growled out loud, recalling the conversation he'd had with his chief the day he'd accepted this assignment.

"I was beginning to think she couldn't make a mistake," Sam had said, confirming that he shared Paul's feelings about the "lady's" amazing infallibility. "But now I think we just might have her. A month ago she hit one of the Bondinni boys out of Detroit. Idiot thought he could cut in on Mangioni territory. Her modus operandi was the same as always, but this time we found a pair of silver wings under the bed. It was the kind of pin worn by airline personnel."

"So you traced it," Paul had prompted, impatient to reach the point where the all the tedious paperwork was finished and his work began.

Sam nodded. "To Trans-National Airlines based out of Minneapolis. It's worn by all of their flight attendants. We cross-checked their flight plans with the killings and guess what?''

"You came up with all the right places and a name?''

"Several names unfortunately, but that's more than we've ever had before,'' Sam replied. "We also discovered that the murders were committed in the hotels most widely used by Trans-National to house their crews, so we've got to be on the right track.''

"Where that woman's concerned, I'm glad to be on any track,'' Paul offered brusquely, recalling the number of organized crime investigations that had been frustrated by the work of the "Scarlet Lady.'' Material witnesses had been eliminated before testifying, gang members had been murdered before turning state's evidence and two of his fellow undercover agents had been hit before they could deliver any damaging information about the Mangioni family.

Mitchell sighed, "You and me both. It's a relief to know our lady didn't just drop in out of thin air, make the hit, then dematerialize. It now appears she was a registered guest and once the dirty deed was done, all she had to do was stroll back to her own room.''

"How convenient,'' Paul bit out acidly. "Give me a name, Sam.''

Mitchell tossed a sheet of paper across his desk. "The computer spit out several names but that's the one who came up most often. We ran a check on her background and learned that she had a college romance with Joseph Mangioni, nephew of Vincent, the man we believe is behind all these contracts. We haven't discovered an underworld connection with any of the other suspects.''

"Anything else?''

"She was born and raised on a farm, which means she'd probably be very familiar with the brand of poison used on the victims. Beyond that, her flight schedules match up almost exactly."

As Paul digested what he'd just been told, Mitchell brought up another intriguing fact. "We had the airlines question their flight personnel, including our suspects, to ascertain whether or not they spent their layover time with other crew members or roomed alone. Supposedly, they were surveying the crews in an attempt to better define some of their staffing problems. One of the women they questioned resigned the very next day. Interesting, huh?"

"Very interesting."

After Mitchell had relayed every scrap of information the bureau had gathered on one Patricia Courteau, Paul recalled the last words he'd said to his chief. "I want her, Sam, and I don't care what I have to do to get her."

What he had to do was pull the wool over the eyes of a sweet old lady who thought the sun rose and set on her granddaughter. That knowledge ate away at him for the rest of the night.

"Best eat another stack of them pancakes, Paul," Aurie advised, passing him the platter. "I don't start on dinner much before noon."

Paul had no choice but to accept the plate thrust under his nose, suppressing a groan as Aurie picked up another. "This here's real Courteau sausage made from our own hogs. Same recipe my mother used and her mother before her. You can tell by the sage. Mama just loved the taste of sage."

Without waiting for Paul's permission, she plunked several more of the greasy, brown links onto his plate, then bustled back to the stove. "Glad to have a man with a decent appetite at the table in the morning. Amos always wolfed down his share but Tricia don't eat enough to keep a body alive. Don't hardly pay to cook like this for her. How d'ya like your eggs?"

"Eggs?" Paul winced at the ominous sound of a carton being opened. "I...eh...don't usually eat eggs and pancakes together, ma'am."

To his relief, Aurie accepted that excuse. "That's fine by me." To his horror, she turned the heat back on under the grill. "Then I'll just keep these pancakes coming."

As soon as Aurie's back was turned, Tricia's eyes were caught by a pair of dazed-looking gray ones. The man looked so desperate that she almost relented and bailed out his protesting stomach, but then she noticed his expensive digital watch. Who was he trying to kid? He couldn't have paid for that on a hired man's salary.

"More syrup, Mr. Lansing?" she inquired graciously, lips twitching. "Grannie makes it herself. If you notice, it's much sweeter and thicker than any you can find in the supermarket."

"No thanks, I've got plenty," he managed, though it took effort to be civil to someone with such a sadistic streak. Behind that Madonna face, Patricia Courteau was enjoying every minute of this torture to his digestive tract. As he surveyed his second stack of thick buttermilk pancakes swimming in maple syrup and the fragrant sausages beside it, the skin around his mouth turned slightly green. He considered his choices and decided he'd be better off offending their over-

generous cook by refusing more of her fare than by
getting sick all over her table.

"I'm sorry, ma'am, but I just can't do justice to this
wonderful breakfast so early in the day," he declared
in defeat, taking another bleary-eyed glance at the
clock over the stove to verify that it was indeed morning. According to his muddled brain, it was still the
middle of the night.

"Why's that?" Aurie's voice held a hint of censure
as she came back to the table to refill Paul's coffee
cup.

"I'm used to eating later, ma'am," he admitted.
"My stomach must still be on my old schedule."

"How strange. The last place you worked served
breakfast after chores?" Tricia asked, her golden
brown eyes alight with seemingly innocent curiosity
and a disgusting amount of vivacity.

"Mmm," Paul grunted noncommittally.

"Didn't you get awfully hungry?" she pursued, a
tiny, catlike smile on her lips. "I know I would. We're
up at six and don't get done with chores much before
eleven. What kind of farm did you say you worked at
last?"

Before answering, Paul took a large swallow of
coffee and burnt his tongue in the process. He almost
dropped the mug as he set it back down on the table
and reached quickly for a glass of milk to soothe the
pain.

"Just brewed a new pot," Aurie announced the
obvious, furrowing her brows as she watched Paul
slosh the cold liquid round in his mouth. "I always
douse hot coffee with cream. Want some in yours?"

Paul shook his head, the wounded expression on his
face masking the satisfaction he felt over bypassing

Patricia's pointed question. Unlike her grandmother, she obviously wasn't going to accept him at face value, but he wasn't up to an inquisition. At this ungodly hour, he was lucky he could move, let alone think straight. "No thanks, ma'am, I shouldn't have taken this cup. I've already had six."

"You're sure now," Aurie questioned when she spied the yawn he couldn't quite hide.

"Yes, ma'am," he assured swiftly. "Six cups ought to be enough to get my motor running. What about you, Patricia? Are you ready to get started on those chores?"

"The name's Tricia and I am if you are," she declared brightly. Standing up from her chair, she thanked her grandmother for breakfast and headed for the porch where all the outdoor gear was stored. She couldn't wait to see how long Paul lasted outside in the freezing cold. His scandalously tight jeans, blue work shirt and brown leather vest looked awfully sexy on him and might raise her temperature a few degrees, but they certainly wouldn't keep him very warm.

She figured it would take about fifteen minutes before he'd retreat back to the house where Grannie would be waiting to loan him a set of Amos's scratchy red long johns, a bulky thermal jacket, woolen muffler and a pair of size-thirteen hobnail boots. That would take care of his exalted position in the sexy department and she could do with the break. With his tousled head of dark sable hair, sulky mouth and mean-machine body, Paul Lansing was much too easy on the eyes.

"Where'd all this stuff come from?" she exclaimed as soon as she stepped into the porch and saw the wide variety of men's clothing hanging on the hooks.

"From the back of my truck. I came prepared for all kinds of weather," Paul told her as he shoved his feet into a pair of fur-lined boots, then reached for a blue, down-filled jacket. He drew an Alpine leaf-patterned tasseled cap out of his pocket and pulled it down over his ears. He didn't notice that Tricia was staring at him as if he'd grown another head until both of his hands were enclosed in rawhide gloves. "Something wrong?"

"You're actually planning to go out dressed like that?"

Paul looked down at himself and frowned. "Why not?"

Tricia didn't know if she should answer truthfully or let him find out for himself. If she didn't place such a high value on her own hard-earned dollars, she just might have opted for the latter. As it was, she couldn't stand by and watch him ruin his expensive clothes, even if he deserved it for posing as an experienced hired hand. "In case you've been misinformed, you aren't going outdoors to impress a bunch of snow-bunnies at a ski lodge, Mr. Lansing. You're going out to tend pigs."

"The name's Paul and I know where I'm going," he corrected her tersely though he couldn't counteract the heat creeping steadily up his cheeks.

"Well, you'll be the best-dressed mucker in the barn."

Paul felt like a fool. He was a fool for making such a stupid blunder. When he'd purchased these clothes, he'd considered their warmth, not whether they were appropriate for the type of work he'd be doing. Worse yet, he'd assumed that everything he needed to know about farming would come back to him without his having to think twice about it. He was beginning to realize that arrogant assumption might land him in real trouble.

"I don't suppose you'd believe that I've wanted to win a prize in that category all my life?" he inquired hopefully.

"I don't suppose I would."

"Didn't think so," he mumbled to himself.

To avoid blowing his cover, a good agent stuck as closely to the truth as possible. Paul decided it was high time he started acting like a good agent. If he didn't want Patricia Courteau labeling him as a total moron, he had some fast talking to do.

He cleared his throat, feigning embarrassment. "Okay, you've got me dead to rights. It's been a while since I've worked on a farm."

"How long of a while?" Tricia asked, surprised by his unexpected show of honesty. She was also touched by the vulnerability she saw in his sleepy gray eyes. It was much easier to remain impervious to a man's charm, even as good-looking a man as Paul Lansing, when he didn't acknowledge any endearing weaknesses.

He smiled sheepishly, "Actually, it's been over twenty years."

"Twenty years! That's a lifetime!"

"Keep your voice down, would you?" Paul cocked his head toward the open door leading back to the kitchen. Actually, he wasn't too worried over Aurie's reaction to his announcement—he'd already won her over—but it might help his cause with Patricia if she thought he was. "Do we have to tell your grandmother?"

Tricia couldn't help it, she was a sucker for that lost puppy dog look. Paul couldn't help but notice the softening in her expression as she said, "If I've figured it out, so has she. This isn't the only mistake you've made."

"It isn't!"

Tricia burst out laughing. He was genuinely astonished to learn that his performance had been less than sterling all along. "Besides your ski-bum outfit, designer jeans and twenty-dollar haircut, you couldn't quite hide your reluctance to get out of bed this morning. Add those things to your distaste for a hearty breakfast and what we've got here is a city slicker posing as a country rube."

Paul was highly insulted by her estimation of his behavior and vexed with himself for overlooking so many telling details. He was a stickler for details, yet he'd practically worn a neon sign proclaiming himself an urbanite. "I wasn't trying to come across as a rube," he protested truthfully.

"Then you must have been born 'yes ma'aming' and 'no ma'aming' everyone to death," she teased.

Becoming more red in the face every second, Paul returned. "And you must have been born with a very suspicious mind."

Tricia's reply was calm, her smile cool. "Where you're concerned, I had good cause to be suspicious, now didn't I?"

Until he'd come up against this woman, Paul had thought that his quick temper had been trained out of him, but it seemed all she had to do to make him break his training was smile at him with that superior little smile.

"Well, didn't I?" she prompted gently.

Paul gritted his teeth, but she kept on smiling and the heat of his temper broke through. In the first unrestrained, completely juvenile gesture he'd made in a very long time, he whisked his hat off his head and threw it on the floor. "So what if I'm not a bona fide farmer, Ms. Goody Goody? If I can do the job, why should you care?"

"I don't," Tricia replied smoothly, taking a step back to avoid getting hit as he started pulling off his jacket. She didn't dare tell him that in her estimation, his self-righteous anger was almost as appealing as his smile. In truth, she was beginning to think that most of his moods looked pretty good on him.

Moreover, she was in dire need of help, experienced or otherwise, a fact she'd somehow managed to forget during her ill-tempered fit of pique last night. "All I wanted to do was stop you from ruining those nice clothes."

Paul was bent down, yanking off his boots when her words finally got through to him. He raised his head. "All you wanted to... huh?"

"Grannie's the boss," Tricia reminded him. "Apparently, she's decided to overlook your inexperience and give you a chance."

Paul straightened up to his full height. For reasons that he'd rather not explore, he needed to know what she thought about him. "What about you, Tricia?"

All at once, Tricia felt as if the spacious back porch had decreased to the size of a small closet and she was trapped inside it with a man who was staring hungrily at her mouth. She swallowed hard, trying not to squirm beneath his heated gaze. "What about me?"

"Are you willing to give me a chance?"

Three

Tricia's mouth went dry at the question and her heart began pounding so fast she couldn't get her breath. Somehow, she had to break the sudden overwhelming sexual tension that strung between them, but her senses went reeling as his mouth curved upward in that lopsided grin that served him so well. She was fast forming a fatal attraction to it, and to those devastating dimples that did exciting little things to her nervous system.

Shaken by that knowledge, she blurted out the first cliché that sprang into her head. "I'm not about to look a gift horse in the mouth."

Since that was exactly what she was doing, Paul couldn't resist pointing it out. "Because you want it?"

"Want what?"

"My mouth."

"What!" Cheeks burning, Tricia realized where her eyes had been glued and what he'd assumed by their unblinking attachment. Even more demoralizing, the assumption was correct. Before matters got entirely out of hand, she had to prove he'd assumed wrong. "We'd better get something straight right now, mister. The only thing you've got that I want is your body!"

As soon as she said it, Tricia realized what she'd said and wished that the floor would open up and swallow her whole. Unfortunately, no such thing happened. Paul crossed his arms over his chest as if he were trying to defend himself from her lecherous attack on his modesty. "I don't know what you've heard, lady, but I'm not that kind of guy," he vowed.

Tricia gave him a dirty look. "You know that wasn't what I meant."

The dimples came back. "Too bad."

"Do you want this job or don't you?" Tricia bit out in frustration and reached for her thermal jacket.

"Sure I do," he assured her, trying his best to combat her doubtful glare. He didn't see the entrancing sparkle in his own eyes or hear the boyish enthusiasm in his voice as he insisted, "Honest, Tricia. I didn't come here just as a favor to your family or because I needed a job. I really want to find out if I'm cut out for this kind of work. You see, I've been thinking about buying my own place. It's kind of a dream of mine. I've got some money saved up and I . . ."

"Okay, okay," she interrupted as soon as she realized that she was hanging on to his every word like an adoring idiot. She could just imagine what he'd do if he noticed that. When he'd noted her interest in his mouth, he'd almost embarrassed her half to death. "I believe you. You don't have to tell me your whole life story."

Tight-lipped, he apologized, "Sorry, I thought you wanted an explanation."

Bent over her boots, Tricia replied in a tone that she hoped conveyed only slight interest, "Some other time, okay? Right now, we've got work to do."

Shortly thereafter, she was all set to go. Paul was still standing there with nothing to wear but the gear he'd just taken off. Heading briskly for the door, she instructed, "Ask Grannie to fix you up with some of Amos's clothes. Whenever you're ready, you can come out and find me in the big barn."

Her voice was curt and dismissive, making Paul feel as if he'd caused a major delay in an airtight schedule. "Tricia, if you wait just a minute, I'll..."

"Hungry piglets wait for no man," she called back over her shoulder as she opened the door and went out.

One minute Paul was pitching soiled straw over the waist-high sides of a ten by twenty foot stall and the next he was standing knee-deep in a moving sea of just weaned Chester Whites. "Dammit!" he swore, trying to maintain his balance as he was caught up in a hairy pink wave of onrushing joy. Tiny ears flapping, eyes expectant and tails atwitter, the pigs rushed for the feeder bins that Tricia had just filled with grain.

"Couldn't you have waited until I was done in here?" he shouted at her as she continued on down the barn's center aisle to the next stall. Over the staccato slamming of the metal feeder lids, the frenetic noises of eating and the sporadic squeal of hungry little pigs chasing other hungry little pigs away from their feeding sites, Paul realized that Tricia was oblivious to his complaint and to his present quandary.

Amos's boots were several sizes too big for him and he risked stepping out of them whenever he moved. Maneuvering his way to the front of the stall without ending up in his stocking feet was going to be a real trick. "Chances are she did this to me on purpose," he grumbled at the milling crowd of porkers butting against his legs.

"That crafty she-devil probably wanted another good laugh at my expense," he muttered darkly, recalling the outburst that had greeted his arrival in the barn.

As soon as he'd changed into Amos Redding's work clothes, he'd known he was in for it. He'd forgotten just how big a man Amos was. He had plenty of room left to spare in the man's jacket, and the hem of his red thermal shirt hung down well over his hips. Of course, Tricia had known all along how poorly the hired man's clothes were going to fit him.

Then, as if the oversize, hobnailed boots, thermal underwear and jacket hadn't been bad enough, Aurie had insisted that his ears and throat needed protection. Before he knew what had hit him, she'd plunked a lumberjack hat with earflaps down on his head and wrapped a thick, hand-knit muffler around his neck. He'd looked like a dwarf pretending to be Paul Bunyan, as Tricia had kindly pointed out the instant she'd clapped eyes on him.

Even after he'd discovered it was plenty warm enough in the barn to do without the jacket, muffler and hat, she still couldn't walk past him without giggling. Hoping to rob her of another chance to make fun of him, Paul slid one foot along the concrete floor and didn't lose a boot. "At this rate, it'll take me five minutes to get out of here," he lamented to no one in particular, and not for the first time decided that it was going to be a very long day.

Tricia was on her way back down the center aisle when she saw one long muscular leg come over the top of a stall. Seconds later, the boot that dangled on the end of that leg fell off to reveal a plaid woolen sock stuffed with the leftover length of Amos's underwear. Expectantly, she waited for the rest of the anatomy to arrive. When it didn't, she set down the buckets of grain she was carrying and started running.

When she reached Paul, he was just about to lose the white-knuckled grip he'd taken on the top rail of the stall. His position resembled that of a broken wishbone, one leg up, one down and bent at the knee. Before he fell backward onto the concrete floor, Tricia jumped up on the bottom rail and flung both arms around his waist. While he struggled to regain his balance, she hung on with all of her might.

"Dammit, woman! You're breaking me in half," Paul swore vehemently as he got a firmer grip on the rail. "Let go of me for Crissakes or we're both going over."

"If I do, you'll really hurt yourself," Tricia warned, her cheek plastered against the warm, woolen underwear that covered his chest. "Grab onto the corner post, then tell me what's got you all hung up like this."

Paul considered his choices and swore again. He'd never thought much about the various means of torture employed through the ages, but if he got out of this alive, he could describe one that should appeal to sadists everywhere. It not only combined being drawn and quartered with the fear of falling, but used a man's natural reaction to having a pair of soft breasts crushed against his hips with the impending threat of castration.

The instant he caught a whiff of Tricia's sweet smelling hair and felt her breath warming his chest through the shirt, he knew he was a goner. "I'm caught on a nail."

"Where?"

"None of your damned business!"

"Oh, there," Tricia murmured knowingly. "Can you keep your balance if I let go of you?"

Paul sighed in resignation. "Yes."

"I'll be gentle," she assured him cheekily as she let go of his waist and bent over the rail.

Paul gritted his teeth as he felt her feeling around the center seam of his jeans. He didn't know where to look. If he looked straight ahead, he got an intimate view of her denim-clad derriere. If he looked down, he saw her head dangling in front of his groin. He quickly revised his earlier opinion. Now this was real torture!

When he heard her mutter, "All the blood's rushing to my head and I can't get this thing loose," he feared correctly that there was worse yet to come. Tricia came back over the stall and went down on her knees on the other side. Paul sucked in his breath when he glanced down and saw her two shapely hands slip through the slot between rails and unsnap his jeans.

"Is this really necessary?" he demanded thickly, trying to keep his voice from creaking like a teenager's as she pulled down his zipper.

"It's not a nail. It's a piece of broken-off barbed wire and...um...it's snagged on your underwear," Tricia noted unsteadily, not too sure her dizziness could be blamed on the time she'd spent hanging head down over the top rail. She was obviously equally embarrassed as he was.

Squeezing her eyes shut, she eased her hand inside his pant leg. She located the rusty barb caught in the ribbed material of his long johns, and began to work it loose.

"If you wanted my body that badly all you had to do was ask," Paul quipped, trying to defuse the tension.

"Thanks," Paul offered as he got himself up and over the rail. Tricia bent down, giving the nasty cause of his dilemma her undivided attention. She wasn't wearing her gloves and didn't have pliers to pull the jagged wire out of the post, but that didn't matter to her. The only thing that mattered was giving them both time to get control of themselves before they had to face each other again.

"No problem," Tricia returned without looking up. "Did it break the skin? If it did you'll need to get a tetanus shot."

Paul stared down at her bent head, prepared to do battle, until he realized that she had no intention of laughing over his predicament. She was blushing! As traumatized by their forced intimacy as he'd been, she was trying to buy herself some time before she had to look him in the face.

Would a woman who made her living going to bed with strange men in order to murder them react this way to what had just happened? Paul didn't think so. As a matter of fact, the more he found out about Patricia Courteau, the more certain he felt that the bureau had sent him after the wrong suspect.

"I've had all my shots," he told her, standing very close to where she was kneeling as he leaned back against the rail to pull on the boot he'd lost over the side.

Tricia nodded at the information, but still refused to show her face.

"Need some help down there?" he inquired courteously.

"No!" she exclaimed, then amended hastily. "That won't solve the problem. It'll take more than bare hands to get this barb out. Why don't you get started on stall six and I'll go find some wire cutters? I don't want one of our valuable animals getting jabbed with this thing."

"God forbid," he asserted dryly.

Tricia did look up then. "I wasn't...of course, I'm sorry for what happened to you, but..."

"I know what you meant." Paul nodded, and managed not to grin at her flushed face. "Stall six, you said?"

"That's the last one that needs cleaning," she asserted quickly, grateful for the return to a safe topic. "Once that's done we can lay down new bedding and call it a morning."

"Okay," he agreed at once, apparently just as anxious as she to put the incident behind them.

Feeling much more friendly toward him and partly responsible for what had just happened, she said, "After lunch, I think we should drive into town and get you some decent work clothes and a pair of boots that fit. You keep slipping in those and I don't want you having another accident."

Paul didn't appreciate her maternal expression. The last think he wanted from her or any woman was her

motherly concern. "Oh, I don't know. I sort of enjoyed the way you came to my rescue."

Mortified all over again, Tricia stammered, "Yes,
well...I'd still like to make sure nothing like that
happens again."

"Not quite like that," he mused suggestively, satisfied by her breathless response and delighted by the
prim and proper streak he'd uncovered in her. It didn't
fit his image of the "Scarlet Lady" at all. She had to
be innocent. She just had to be and if she was...

"Shall we get back to work, Mr. Lansing?"

"By all means, Miss Courteau." Paul reached down
and grasped her elbow, assisted her to her feet, then
stuffed his hands in his pockets to keep them in line.
Whenever she was within touching distance, he had to
fight the urge to pull her into his arms and kiss her.
Under the circumstances, acting on that urge would
not only be foolhardy, but also premature until he had
irrefutable evidence that she was just as she seemed.
No matter how tempted he was by her, he had to remember that he still hadn't proved anything one way
or the other.

Tricia kept a wary eye on him as he shuffled his way
down the center aisle toward stall six, not knowing
what to make of him or her overwhelming response to
being near him. As a flight attendant, she was familiar with every type of man there was and knew how to
fend off the most flirtatious lines tossed her way. Why,
then, was she having such a difficult time with this
man?

She'd seen square jaws, white teeth and dimples before. She'd seen broad shoulders and long legs and
every kind of gorgeous muscle known to man. So what
was her problem?

She prayed her attraction wasn't as obvious to him as it was to her, but according to the jaunty tune he was whistling, she didn't think her prayers had been heard. Paul Lansing was trouble with her name spelled on it and at this unsettled point in her life, the last thing she needed was more trouble.

Quitting her job hadn't been that difficult for her to do, but she'd hoped to be much further along with her plans for her own business by now. She'd been back on the farm a whole month and still hadn't made her first contact with a possible consignor or established herself as an agent for their goods. First, she'd had to tend to her grandmother until she'd recovered from the crippling arthritis that acted up every winter and then Amos had been called away to his brother's bedside, which had left her doing all the chores.

For the last two weeks, instead of having the time to seek out and find the kind of items she wanted to market and sell, she'd rarely gotten a good night's sleep. She'd chased back and forth to the doctor for Grannie's medicine. She'd chased to town for groceries and supplies. She'd chased after what seemed like hundreds of pigs and then, to top it off, last night she'd gone chasing after a pack of marauding stray dogs.

If Paul Lansing had turned out to be the common, everyday variety of hired man, she'd have greeted his arrival as a godsend. As it was, though she could kick herself for doing so, he was just one more thing she found herself chasing after. All she could do was pray that he wouldn't make matters even worse by turning around and letting himself get caught. She had no idea what she'd do about it if he did. She didn't even want

to think about the upheaval that it might cause in her
life.

So I won't, she promised silently and didn't allow
herself a single glance in his direction as she passed by
him on her way through the doorway to the attached
shed where they stored feed, tools and medicinal supplies. Once inside, she prepared a dosage of medica-
tion for a litter of nine. She was filling a disposable
syringe when Paul joined her.

"What are you doing?" he demanded.

Tricia was startled by his sharp tone and he must
have realized how he'd sounded for he immediately
explained the motive behind his question. "Are you
experienced at giving injections? Doesn't the vet normally handle that kind of thing?"

"Twenty years ago maybe, but not anymore. We
can't afford to call the vet out here every time there's
a new litter," she replied, pointing to the vials of pre-
prepared mixture they used to inoculate all their new-
borns. The expression that came over his face when he
read the scientific-sounding label amused her. "Don't
look so worried. I know what I'm doing."

He didn't seem very reassured by her confident
statement and followed closely at her heels as she carried the tray of syringes back into the barn. If he
hadn't told her how long it had been since he'd been
on a farm, she would've been irritated by his attitude
as she entered the stall. "As long as you're here, why
don't you make yourself useful and hold this tray for
me?" she requested, shaking her head when he
stopped dead in his tracks. "Look, if you don't want
to watch this, I'm not forcing you."

"Give me the tray," he bit out tersely, practically
yanking it out of her hands.

More confused than ever by his odd behavior, Tricia gave up trying to figure him out and reached under the heat lamp for a tiny, pink piglet. "I'm not about to commit murder," she couldn't resist saying when she noted his grim expression. "I'm doing it for their own good. Baby pigs are subject to all sorts of diseases this one little shot can prevent."

By the time she'd injected the ninth of the litter, Tricia had concluded that Paul had some kind of a neurotic fear of needles. His face was very pale and she saw that his hands were trembling when she placed the last empty syringe on the tray. Since she wasn't that fond of needles herself and did everything in her power to avoid the doctor's office, he had her sympathy.

She met his intent gaze over the tray as she took it back from him. "I've gotten to be such an expert at this that they don't even notice when the nee—what I'm doing.

"See, there," she gestured over her shoulder to the row of sleeping babies. "Most of them didn't even wake up and those that did are already snoozing again."

"You've an expert hand all right," he said, verifying the piglets' unharmed condition, but his voice still sounded strange.

"I won't ask you to do any inoculations," she informed him gently. "I can tell that it bothers you."

He held her eyes for what seemed like an eternity before conceding, "Yes, it does. It bothers me quite a bit."

Two hours later, seated beside Paul in his truck, Tricia was still being given the silent treatment. The man had hardly spoken a word to her as they'd finished chores and gone back to the house. During lunch, he'd only spoken when he'd had to; he had been so deep in thought at times that Grannie had asked him if he had trouble with his hearing.

When Tricia had announced that they were going into town to get him some decent work clothes, he'd volunteered to drive, but that conversation had been about as short-lived as the one she'd attempted when they'd started down the road. Getting nothing in return but one syllable answers, she'd finally gotten the message and for the last several miles, they'd driven along in silence.

Tricia couldn't imagine the kind of childhood trauma that might have prompted such an irrational reaction in him, and didn't dare ask. She did know that they'd never be able to work together if he planned to continue giving her the cold shoulder. No matter what he may have suffered in the past, she didn't deserve being punished for it. "All I did was inoculate nine piglets, not commit some heinous crime!"

She'd intended to get his attention, but Paul was so startled that he almost drove the pickup into the ditch. "Are you trying to get us both killed?" he yelled back at her, needing both hands to regain control of the swerving wheels. The next thing he knew, his brakes locked and the truck fishtailed across the slippery road and into a snowbank. "Of all the stupid...idiotic...lame-brained—"

"Unqualified, ill-prepared drivers, I've ever met you take the cake," Tricia concluded his tirade. "If you never learned how to drive on ice, why didn't you just say so and I would've driven?"

It took Paul a full minute to get his mouth closed and during the entire time, Tricia just sat there and stared at him, arms crossed over her chest, head cocked to one side in a questioning pose. "Hmm?"

Paul gazed into her shameless brown eyes and found himself fighting down the urge to laugh. He could tell that she was doing the same thing, but he refused to break down first, not when she was so obviously gloating over her ability to turn the tables on him. The need to kiss that smug look off her face was almost overpowering.

"Do you know what you deserve, young lady?" he inquired curtly, doing his damnedest to keep his dishonorable intentions a secret from her until he was ready to act.

Composing her features, Tricia replied loftily, "No, but if you'd like to tell me, I'll be more than happy to listen. Unlike you, I believe it's essential for two people who work together to establish and maintain open lines of communication."

"I haven't been holding up my end of things, is that it?" he inquired after a thoughtful pause.

"No, you haven't."

Paul leaned back, smiling at her as he slid his arm along the top of the seat. "Then I apologize for my surly behavior."

"Apology accepted." Tricia returned his smile. "And I apologize for the outburst that landed us in the ditch."

He nodded graciously, then hit her with the full force of his dimples. Tricia was so enthralled, she didn't even notice that his face was much too close to hers until he lifted his hand and smoothed his thumb across her breathlessly parted lips. She felt the tingle all the way to her toes.

Paul looked down at her soft, full mouth, outlined with a delicate shade of pink, and his arm slid down the seat and around her shoulders. "You have my promise that from here on in, I'll make every effort to keep our lines of communication open," he murmured in a deep whisper, threatening her mouth with his, yet not coming close enough to take it. "All you had to do was ask."

She neither realized that she was instinctively adjusting herself to his hold, nor that she was prepared to ask for anything he might care to give her, until she heard her own whispered "please," and then it was too late.

Paul lowered his head and kissed her.

She momentarily held her breath, then released it, swallowing hard. When he lifted his mouth away, she emitted a soft moan. She wanted him, and now he knew how much.

"Me, too," he murmured, before bringing his mouth down on hers again.

Tricia's lips parted even as he touched them. His mouth was every bit as wonderful as she'd imagined and every bit as experienced. His lips coaxed and incited, explored and demanded, but somehow she managed to hold her own. She returned every movement, challenged him and accepted his challenge as her tongue traced the hard line of his lips in ways she'd never wanted to try with anyone else. With him, she was wildly, excitingly curious and it brought about a response that shocked them both.

Paul groaned deep in his throat as her arms came up around his neck and her fingers caressed his nape. She was so soft, so warm and willing for him, he was burning up. Every taut muscle, every inflamed nerve in his body demanded that he pull her down on top of him and relieve the ache. But he couldn't; no matter how much he wanted her, he couldn't take her. Not yet, and not like this, in the front seat of a battered pickup.

Even so, his body craved more satisfaction than it was getting and he couldn't seem to combat it. His hands moved between their bodies and found the zipper of her jacket. The buttons of her blouse were dispensed with soon after. The instant his fingers made contact with her bare skin, he was too far gone to question who or what she might be. The only thing that mattered was how she felt and how she made him feel.

Don't think about this. Don't question, Tricia commanded herself, for if she allowed her rational brain to reclaim control, she couldn't enjoy what was happening and the pleasure was too great to even think of denying herself. He cupped her breasts gently, as if they were fragile blossoms, while his thumbs caressed the throbbing tips to tight buds.

She bit her lip to keep from crying out as he brought his fingers into play. Instinct took over and she arched her back, overcome by sensation as he kneaded and stroked her, setting a rhythm they both desired with increasing urgency.

Paul heard a sound from Tricia, so sweet, so unbearably sweet, that it reached a place inside him that had never been touched by a woman before. The amount of feeling contained in that sound frightened him, and that stopped him as nothing else could have.

He couldn't handle such feelings in himself, let alone be responsible for inspiring them in someone else.

It took every ounce of willpower he had, but his fingers stopped caressing her tempting curves and moved quickly to eliminate all further temptation. Before Tricia was aware that the wondrous sensations had ceased, her blouse was buttoned and her jacket zipped.

In a daze, she gazed up at him, her eyes so beseeching they were almost Paul's undoing. "We're in a truck for heaven sakes. I don't know about you, but I gave up these kinds of gymnastics over twenty years ago."

The reality of their behavior set in with a vengeance and Tricia couldn't get back to her own side of the seat fast enough. She covered her face with her hand so she couldn't read what had almost happened in his eyes.

Paul forced himself to move away from her, catching a glance of his slightly swollen mouth in the rearview mirror as he slid back behind the wheel. He took an unsteady breath, liking the sight of her mark on him, liking it too much for his own peace of mind. He looked over at her, wishing he could deny that the thought of his mark on her lips and on those beautiful breasts of hers didn't give him an even greater amount of pleasure.

Still shaking in reaction, Tricia needed all her courage for even one glance across the space that separated them.

It was silent for a moment, until Paul turned toward her, his gray eyes flashing. "I don't think communication is going to be a problem with us, do you?"

Four

Thanks for the help, Mr. Anderson," Tricia shouted to be heard over the engine of the tractor. The farmer doffed his cap at her before steering the tractor back down the gravel road toward his barn. With great reluctance, Tricia turned to face the truck that was now free to go along on its merry way and to the less than merry-looking man waiting beside it.

"It's a good thing he saw us," Paul said as she approached. "All I had to dig us out was my bare hands."

Wishing to forego her involvement in anything that had transpired over the last twenty minutes, Tricia was glad to embrace the mundane. "The next time you're on the road under icy conditions you should carry a shovel along and sandbags for ballast. Then, even if you get stuck, you can pour out the sand under your wheels and get some traction. I've got studded tires on my car and chains in the trunk. When the snowplow's slow in coming, I can still get through on most of these back roads."

"Sounds like good advice," Paul replied, but couldn't resist tacking on, "Though I wouldn't have needed chains, sand bags or a cold shower if I'd left you at home."

"That would've been fine with me," Tricia retorted feelingly, despising him for reminding her of something she wanted to forget in the worst way. She'd also like to ignore the fact that he couldn't be held responsible for her sex-starved response to his kisses. If he chose to bring up the humiliating subject every minute of every day, she had no one to blame but herself.

The knowledge that she hadn't been satisfied with mere kissing, but had practically begged him to do more was humiliating. If Paul hadn't put a stop to things when he had, she would've willingly had sex with him in the cab of his pickup. The image made her stomach churn and brought a flush to her cheeks.

Even as a teenager out on a date to the local drive-in, she'd never gone in for the heavy petting her dates expected to take place in the back seat. Yet, here she was at the worldly age of thirty-two, ready and willing to go "all the way" with a man she knew next to nothing about. Incredible she thought darkly to herself, unable to blot out the picture of Paul's hands on her bare breasts. The man had accomplished more in one day than half the adolescent boys in Jackson county, several young men at the state college and a goodly number of Trans-National passengers had been able to do in two decades.

With the exception of Joe Mangioni, the one man she'd ever considered marrying, she'd never gone much beyond kissing. She'd met Joe in her freshman year at college and had swallowed every word of his romantic lines. Within a month, she'd agreed to move in with him, believing his promise that they'd soon be married. Joe had taught her the difference between having sex and making love and she'd learned the lesson the hard way. Right then and there, she'd decided that she'd never again get involved with a man who talked about love but only wanted a convenient outlet for his sexual drive.

If she ever got engaged again, she planned to make sure that the feelings she had about love, marriage and family commitment were well matched. That idealistic notion had kept her single far longer than Grannie Aurie cared to accept. Not before or since her relationship with Joe had she found one man who shared her old-fashioned outlook on intimacy.

Paul Lansing certainly didn't, but that hadn't stopped her from giving up every one of her lofty principles in order to feel his marvelous hands on her body. Love had had nothing whatsoever to do with it. For all her fine ideals, she'd settled for a cheap thrill in the front seat of a truck like a real, card-carrying floozy. If Grannie ever found out about this, she'd throw ten fits and if her broom was any place handy, the first blow would send Paul Lansing into the next county!

As they got back into the truck and continued on to Quincy, Tricia was so wrapped up in her own turbulent feelings that she barely noticed that Paul seemed to be just as upset by their encounter as she was. This time the silence between them was by mutual agree-

ment. She was glad not to talk and prayed the silence
would last until she could get some perspective on
what had just happened, then figure out a means of
preventing it from ever happening again.

Unfortunately, whenever she thought about the way
his hungry mouth had felt on hers, the hard thrust of
his body against her quivering softness, all she could
think about was what it would be like if they "com-
municated" on the most intimate level possible. In
self-disgust, she had to admit that her recent indulg-
ence in raw, primitive lust was the most exciting thing
that had ever happened to her.

Paul held off as long as he could, but finally glanced
at the woman seated next to him to see if she was far-
ing any better than he was. She wasn't. He noted the
flush on her cheeks, the rapid rise and fall of her full
breasts beneath her jacket and swiftly glanced away,
reading her mind. For an Iowa farm girl, she was the
hottest little number he'd ever met, which led him to
believe she'd learned quite a bit since leaving the farm.

He wondered how many other men had wanted her
as he had and how many had gotten what they wanted.
If she responded to every man as she'd responded to
him, he was sure she'd led a very active social life. As
a flight attendant, she'd traveled the world. For all he
knew, she could have a lover in every city where Trans-
National flew.

The "Scarlet Lady" had the ability to draw men like
bees to a sweet smelling garden and he couldn't deny
that Patricia Courteau had the same talent. He'd been
forewarned and he still couldn't keep his hands off
her. She was like a beautiful, exotic flower, exuding a
fragrance that was irresistible to men. Whenever he
was near her, he felt the pull on his senses and it was

growing stronger all the time. He wanted to reach for that flower, strip away every deceptively fragile petal until he found the very essence of her.

She wanted that, too. Paul gripped the wheel so hard his knuckles went white but his mind refused to stay on his driving. "If you don't stop dwelling on what almost happened, it still might!" He bit off the words, feeling as if he were about to explode.

"Not if I have anything to say about it," Tricia shot back, needing an outlet for her own frustrations and deciding he was the perfect target. "I'll admit I'm attracted to you, but hell will freeze over before I take up with any hired man."

Paul laughed out loud at her archaic phrasing. "Take up? Now there's a genteel description for something that wouldn't be the least bit refined if you make love like you kiss. You've got a wild, little tongue, sweetheart."

Tricia was too shocked and ashamed to respond to that, but Paul mistook her silence for something else. He assumed she was the type who felt herself above such a crude urge as lust, but wasn't above teasing a man into a sexual frenzy. That kind of "lady," he did his best to avoid.

He was curious to know how this one planned to rationalize her recent behavior. If that wasn't lust, he didn't know what was, and he knew any number of women who'd consider him an expert on the subject.

Then another theory came to him. The "Scarlet Lady" understood all there was to understand about male lust and she knew exactly how to use it to her best advantage. Had the last man who'd died by her hand heard those sweet little sounds he'd heard just before she'd . . . ?

Paul couldn't finish the thought, but lashed out at the woman beside him because of it. "Lady, you might not like the idea of *taking up* with a hired man, but you would have taken it all off for this one, if I hadn't turned down your offer."

"If you had one decent bone in your body, you wouldn't throw that in my face," Tricia accused bitterly, on the verge of tears. "I'm well aware that I threw myself at you and believe me, you can't be half as disgusted with my behavior as I am. I don't know what came over me . . . I . . . just . . ." Her voice trailed away as the humiliated tears spilled over onto her cheeks.

Disgusted? Disgust was the last thing he'd felt when he'd touched her but he doubted she'd stop crying if he told her what had really been going on in his mind. If he outlined all the things he'd like to do to her body, she might get hysterical. And he certainly couldn't tell her that she was under suspicion of murder. After firing him, Sam Mitchell would have his hide. So what could he say?

"You know damned well what came over you," he declared gruffly. "And I enjoyed it immensely, so you can knock off the act."

When Tricia emitted a tiny moan and cried all the harder, Paul felt like a louse. He didn't have the first idea how to handle a woman in tears, especially one who was crying her heart out because she genuinely believed she'd done something immoral by enjoying his caresses. Her distress wasn't an act. She couldn't fake those dainty hiccups and indelicate sniffs and she'd hate for any man to see the unbecoming red blotches under her eyes.

Every tear that rolled down her face increased his guilt, yet warmed something inside him that had been cynical and cold for more years than he cared to count. With a runny nose and blotchy skin, Patricia Courteau touched his heart and he knew deep down inside himself that she was a lady, a real, honest-to-goodness lady—one of the few he'd ever met.

"I . . . I've never acted that way before," Tricia whispered brokenly, and averted her face, aware that she was making a total fool of herself, but unable to stop crying. It was as if the emotional stress and physical exhaustion of the last several weeks had finally caught up with her, and she'd cracked under the strain. She wasn't even sure that her wanton behavior with Paul was the main cause of her tears. It was just the last in a series of events that had left her feeling as if she had no real control over what was happening to her.

It wasn't that she regretted her decision to leave her job. She'd been thinking about starting her own business for a long time. Nor did she resent her grandmother for always relying on her to intercede with her parents whenever their opinions clashed. She loved all of them and understood where both sides were coming from.

But then Amos had left and all the farm work had fallen on her shoulders. Her parents had immediately started complaining that her grandmother was taking advantage of her good nature. Whenever Tricia spoke to them, they tried their hardest to convince her that selling the farm and moving Grannie into a home would be best for all concerned. And they poured on the guilt by saying that with the economy in such bad shape, they could certainly use the extra income gleaned from the sale.

Furthermore, her father didn't have any confidence in Tricia's ability to build a successful business for herself when she was also responsible for every emergency that came up on the farm. He was quick to remind her that Amos's departure was only one example of the kinds of things that could go wrong from day to day. With prices for pork so depressingly low, the farm couldn't survive too many losses and then where would they all be?

As for her mother, Leona couldn't get over the fact that her daughter had given up her glamorous, well-paying job with the airlines in the hope of selling hand-painted pickle jars to city dwellers. Since Tricia had yet to even get started on that dubious occupation, Leona wanted to know how long she planned to postpone her own goals to meet the needs of a selfish old woman who'd do her darndest to keep Tricia from ever leaving the old homestead.

It seemed as if her whole family was up in arms and she was caught in the middle. Then Paul Lansing had arrived with his big, strong body and "come hither" smile. She'd accepted his presence out of desperation, trying to stay immune to his personal charm, but then he'd turned up the heat and she'd joined what she suspected was a very long list of accommodating women.

Now she had another battle on her hands, a fight within herself. It was just too much for any one person to handle, and this crying jag proved it. But enough was enough, she decided, blowing her nose on a pitifully small scrap of Kleenex she'd found in her jeans.

Starting tomorrow, there's going to be some changes made! she promised herself and let the cathartic tears flow.

Paul cleared his throat, dug in his pockets for a handkerchief and came up empty. He turned on the radio and fiddled with the dials. He stared out the windshield to his left, never to his right, and wondered if they'd ever get to a town called Quincy. When he saw the sign that proclaimed their arrival, he wondered what he was going to do if Tricia hadn't stopped crying by the time he found a place to park.

He needn't have worried. When he'd backed into a place on the main street and had little left to do but turn off the engine, Tricia had an awkward little speech all ready for him. "Destry's clothing store is down the block to the right. I have to pick up a few things, too, so we can go our separate ways."

She paused for only a second, but he heard the tiny catch in her voice as she requested, "If it's all right with you, we can meet back here in about an hour?"

"Of course, that's all right with me. Tricia, I . . ."

"Fine," she cut him off as she opened the door and hopped out of the truck. "Then I'll see you back here at three."

Hating himself for hurting her, Paul stared after her until she disappeared round the nearest corner and kept his eyes glued to that spot for several minutes afterward. Then, his features impassive, he got out of the truck and went looking for a phone booth. He found one in the drugstore, wedged between the magazine stand and a rack of disposable diapers.

As soon as he heard the click on the other end of the line, he launched into his attack without bothering to identify himself. "Damn your computers, Mitchell. If she's a cold-blooded killer, I'm the king of Siam! She's good people, now get me the hell out of here!''

"Great! That was fast work,'' Sam Mitchell enthused, making no comment on his agent's disregard for standard operating procedures. ''If you've got the proof, I'll wire you a fast ticket out of town.''

A few moments later, he realized that the silence he was hearing wasn't due to any lag time on the long distance wires. ''You do have proof, Lansing?''

''You'll just have to take my word for it.''

''Sorry, pal, that won't go over well in my report. I'll need a few corroborating facts.''

''The fact is she's innocent,'' Paul insisted stubbornly, and he meant that in more ways than one.

''No familiar-sounding drugs in the barn?''

Silence.

''We've got reason to believe there are a few more bodies that can be laid at her doorstep,'' Chief Mitchell continued relentlessly. ''We now suspect that before she turned her hand to poison, she used a gun with a very effective silencer. Have you discovered that the Courteau woman wouldn't know which end of a gun was up?''

Silence.

''What about the Mangioni connection? Is that circumstantial?''

''It can't be any anything else. I'm not sure they ever even made it to bed. The way she...''

''The way she what?''

Paul ignored the question. ''Okay, I can't prove that her relationship with Vincent's nephew wasn't anything serious, but I'd stake my badge on it.''

''You might have to if it turns out that you're wrong,'' Mitchell stated bluntly. ''What explanation does she have for leaving Trans-National the day after she was queried on her work schedules for the dates and times in question?''

"She came home to look after her grandmother."

"Uh huh," Mitchell sighed reflectively, beginning to think that his top agent was in very serious trouble. "Sounds to me like you've come to these conclusions by using something other than your head."

"You've never doubted my instincts before," Paul replied sullenly.

"You've never given me cause before," Mitchell reminded. "You always had evidence to back up your theories. This isn't like you Paul. Maybe you'd better tell me what's going on out there."

"You want evidence, Chief? I'll get you all the damned evidence you need!" Paul vowed tightly, then slammed the phone back on its hook.

Destry's department store provided a very disgruntled male customer with the clothing he wanted in about twenty minutes, which left Paul with a half hour to explore the rest of the small town. Since the entire place was three blocks long and composed of about six brick buildings, two of which were bars, the process took him less than fifteen minutes. He returned to the truck prepared for a wait and was surprised to find Tricia already there.

"Are you ready to go?" he inquired tentatively as he opened the door and slid behind the wheel.

"All set," she replied in a bright and surprisingly firm voice. "How about you?"

"Destry's took care of everything on my list," he said, giving her a narrow-eyed glance before turning the key in the ignition. She'd made up her mind about something, Paul was sure. He also sensed that whatever it was she'd decided was going to affect him in a way he probably wasn't going to like. Her big beautiful eyes were still slightly red-rimmed, but other than that there was no sign that she'd been crying.

Actually, she looked all revved up and raring to go and he didn't think it had anything to do with their return trip to the farm. If he wasn't so terrified of making her cry again, he'd demand to know what it did have to do with. The lady had a very determined gleam in her eye.

They were five miles down the highway when Paul heard a soft, mournful whine. He turned his head sharply, but the sound hadn't come from the woman beside him. When he saw where it did come from, his eyes went very wide and a large lump formed in his throat. "Where'd you get that?" he croaked.

Tricia bent down and picked up the snub-nosed, chocolate-brown puppy out of the small cardboard box wedged between her feet. "Isn't he cute?" she asked, as the small animal snuggled down on her lap and promptly went to sleep. "We think he's a full-blooded Labrador retriever."

"Who's we?"

"Our postman, Gordy Mills and I," Tricia said, as her fingers gently stroked the bundle of soft, sleeping fur. "Gordy found him and two other newborn pups in a box by the side of the road a little ways outside of town. They were probably tossed out of the car. Gordy fed them by hand, but this little guy was the only one of three who lived."

"Why didn't Gordy keep him?" Paul asked in a tone that Tricia had never heard him use before.

"Gordy's got five dogs already," she informed him, studying the strange expression on his face. "Don't you like dogs?"

He didn't answer for the longest time and when he did, his voice was tight and there was a faraway look in his eyes. "I had a dog just like that once, a chocolate Lab. I called him Smokey."

"That's a good name," she said, looking down at the plump brown puppy in her lap. "He looks like a pint-sized Smokey the Bear. Would you mind if I called him Smokey, too?"

Tricia didn't think Paul heard the question. He was lost in some memory, a touching earnestness in his expression. "Smokey hated being tied up. One time he ate a baby pine tree to get loose. I swatted him with a newspaper to teach him that trees weren't part of a good canine diet and he ate the paper."

Tricia giggled at the picture he described, but her laughter drained away when she noted the sadness in his eyes. "How old were you when Smokey died?"

"I don't know when he died," he admitted hoarsely. "I left home when I was sixteen and I never went back. I wanted to take him with me, but by then he'd lost his eyesight and most of his hearing."

He seemed to be struggling to get the words out. She saw him swallow hard and she rushed to reassure him. "I'm sure you felt he was much better off where he was."

"That wasn't it," Paul muttered bleakly and Tricia sensed that a wealth of pain backed up each word. "My dad got Smokey for me on my sixth birthday. I found him sleeping on the end of my bed when I woke up. He wasn't allowed back in the house after that day, but we were still almost inseparable from then on. I thought if I left him behind, Dad would feel like a part of me was still there. It wasn't his fault that I had to go. I loved our farm and my dad but I couldn't stay there when she—'' Paul stopped himself in midsentence, suddenly realizing that he was about to tell Patricia something he'd never told another living soul.

Acutely uncomfortable, he glanced over at her. Tricia gazed back at him, no more able to hide the compassion in her eyes than he could hide the sadness in his. All of her maternal instincts made her want to comfort him, to pull his head down on her breast and speak softly until he felt secure enough to tell her the cause of his pain.

She didn't do any of those things, sensing that he'd reject any attempt on her part to mother him. The "she" Paul mentioned with such bitterness could only be his mother and it was plain that the woman had caused a boy of sixteen to leave home for good. It was just as apparent that Paul still suffered a great deal of torment over that decision, but didn't want to talk about it.

To get them both past the tense moment, Tricia said in an even tone, "You didn't answer my question."

Paul was staring straight ahead and she heard the wariness in his tone as he asked, "What question?"

"Would you mind if I called this little guy Smokey? I think it's the perfect name for him."

Tricia saw his jaw work and immediately made herself busy rearranging her jacket around the warm body in her lap. She looked up when he spoke, but gave nothing more than a pleased smile when he said, "No, I wouldn't mind."

Tricia lifted a small, brown leg. "Will you look at the size of these paws? He could very well grow up to be the size of a bear."

Paul grinned, but then his expression changed to one of concern. "Does your grandmother know you're bringing him home?"

Tricia nodded, sensing what had inspired the question and anxious to put his mind at ease. "As long as I've known her, Grannie's always had a dog. Her last one died of old age about three months ago. Shep was her faithful companion and she said she wouldn't get another one. She always says that. But last week she went to the post office and Gordy just happened to have Smokey sitting on the counter. It was love at first sight."

The minute they arrived back at the farm, Paul discovered that Tricia was right on target concerning Aurie's feelings. The elderly woman must have been watching for their arrival for as soon as they got out of the truck, she was yelling out the door. "Tuck that baby inside your jacket so he don't take cold. Didn't that Gordy give you a blanket or anything? Hurry up now, I can see the poor thing shiverin' from here. I've got his first meal all ready for him."

Tricia shot Paul an I-told-you-so look. "There's one really good thing about bringing a new puppy into this house."

"What's that?"

"She'll spend more time fussing over him than fussing over us. Sometimes she treats me like I'm still in diapers."

Paul laughed, remembering the muffler and hat he'd been forced to wear to the barn. "I felt the same way when she made sure that the only thing showing when I left the house this morning was my eyes."

"Try going without your boots sometime and see what happens. Like it or not, once Grannie's accepted you into her house, you're considered part of the family and that means you have to answer to her if you don't tow the line," Tricia warned. "I'd advise you to clean your plate at supper tonight. She took it easy on you this morning, but you won't get away with that again."

Paul groaned, picturing the gigantic portions he'd been served at breakfast and knowing he wouldn't be able to do justice to half that amount of food if faced with it again.

Tricia didn't display the slightest sympathy for his plight, but jabbed him in the ribs. In a voice very much like her grandmother's, she declared, "Goin' to fatten you up, boy. I don't know whose been feeding you but you're nothin' but bones. Eat up now, every speck of food on that plate or I'll know the reason why."

"Will you two stop your dawdling!" Aurie called out the door. "You can flirt just as well inside a warm house."

It was Tricia's turn to groan as the man next to her broke into loud, uninhibited laughter.

Five

Tricia sighed in resignation as she walked into the living room and saw that Grannie had already nodded off in her rocking chair and Paul was stretched out on the couch. Her gaze lingered for a moment on the sleeping man, smiling as she spotted the fat brown puppy curled up on his chest. Though she disliked the thought of putting off what she wanted to say until morning, she didn't know if she had the heart to wake him. He looked so peaceful and relaxed, and there was something about him that made her think he didn't relax very often.

At supper he'd given them a brief, but telling description of his background. After serving four years in the army, he'd taken several varied jobs in several varied locations across the country. He'd worked in construction in Arizona, as a truck driver out of Los Angeles and once when he'd been really down on his luck, he'd taken a job as a fry cook at a cheap diner in Detroit. When he'd first met James Redding, he'd been working as an auto mechanic in a small garage outside Pittsburg.

He'd taken Amos up on his proposition to hire himself on at their farm because he'd always had it in his mind to someday have his own place and he wanted to see what it would be like. After years of being on someone else's payroll, he also liked the idea of being his own boss and at thirty-eight, he felt it was time he thought about settling down.

Finding out that Paul had rarely stayed long in one spot came as no surprise to Tricia. From the start, she'd sensed a certain restlessness in him and was sure that before too long, he'd give up the idea of buying his own piece of land. Paul Lansing was a loner, a drifter with itchy feet, and he couldn't settle down if he tried. She'd be wise to remember that in the future and do her best to counteract her attraction to him. No matter how contented he looked at the moment, he just wasn't the hearth and home type.

Any type might succumb to the relaxing atmosphere of Grannie's living room. With a fire crackling in the old stone fireplace, a lacy layer of frost on the large bay windows and the mantle clock ticking away the evening hours, the room had a warm and homey feel. After a day of hard work and a hot, filling supper, Tricia knew how tempting it was to doze off in a comfortable, overstuffed chair. Unfortunately, she'd rarely had time to enjoy that luxury since coming back home.

Grannie didn't ask for any concessions on account of her age or health, but Tricia knew that she just didn't have the physical stamina she'd once had. Tricia pretended not to notice, but she was well aware of the frequent catnaps Grannie snuck in during the day. Even with those short rests, it was all Grannie could do to fix a light supper and stay awake long enough to eat it, which was why Tricia had taken on the task of cleaning up afterward. Paul's arrival had only added to that burden, for Grannie was raised to believe that a man needed three square meals a day.

As a rule, Amos had taken his evening meal with a bunch of his old cronies over at Millie's Diner. Somehow Tricia doubted that Paul would develop a similarly romantic interest in the sixty-year-old femme fatale who owned the local eatery. That meant Tricia would be doing extra dishes every night.

Thinking back on their recent meal and the amount of time she'd spent in the kitchen clearing away the remnants, Tricia felt less and less guilty about waking Paul. She might not be able to change Grannie's old-fashioned ideas about the division of roles between the sexes, but that didn't mean she had to share them. She'd worked just as long and hard as Paul had today and it wasn't fair that she had to slave over a pile of dirty pots and pans while he took a nap on the couch.

With renewed determination, Tricia sat down in an upholstered chair that was placed halfway between the couch and the rocker. Since Grannie nodded off at the drop of a hat and woke up just as easily, Tricia didn't worry about gaining her attention. Her efforts were directed at the sleeping man on the couch.

First she cleared her throat, then she coughed and when neither of those tactics worked, she started humming. The puppy woke up when she lifted a newspaper off the coffee table and started rattling the pages, but Paul didn't so much as flinch. Nor did he

open his eyes when she started drumming her finger-
nails on the wooden arms of her chair.

"Well, you've certainly got my attention," Aurie
remarked dryly. "But it looks like it might take a stick
of dynamite to get his. That poor man must really be
tired. Maybe you should just let him sleep."

"We're not paying him to sleep. We're paying him
to work," Tricia said, surprising her grandmother with
her vehemence. The elderly woman was even more
astonished when Tricia got up from her chair,
marched over to the couch and began shaking Paul's
arm. "Wake up," she ordered. "I want to talk to
you."

"Mmm hmm," Paul mumbled, snuggling down
further in the soft cushions. Tricia scowled and Grannie laughed, but a second later, they were both wearing the same stunned expression.

"Goodness me!" Aurie exclaimed as she viewed
Tricia's prone body on the carpet and the man who
was lying on top of her with one forearm pressed
across her throat.

Tricia might have made a similar exclamation if the
weight of Paul's chest on her lungs and his arm across
her throat wasn't cutting off her air supply. That being
the case, all she could manage was a tiny, protesting
squeak, and a pleading stare as she struggled to get out
from under him.

It took Paul several moments to recover his whereabouts and when he did, he was horrified. Patricia
Courteau was exactly where he most wanted her to be,
squirming beneath him, but she hadn't arrived in the
position willingly. "Geez, I'm sorry," he mumbled,
still half in a daze as he stared down into her beautiful brown eyes. "You must have startled me."

"I think she'd appreciate your apology a little more, young man, if you weren't choking off her air," Aurie pointed out logically, an amused twinkle in her eyes as Paul's face flooded with color and he hurried to correct the situation. Occupying one of the best seats in the house, Aurie watched the proceedings and tried to remember when she'd last enjoyed such delightful entertainment.

By the time she'd been assisted into a standing position, Tricia's face was as red as that of the man who'd belatedly managed to lever his muscular body off of hers. During the clumsy process, she'd obtained an explicit accounting of his form and she was certain he'd acquired a similar amount of information concerning hers. To make matters worse, Grannie Aurie had cackled gleefully throughout the entire process.

As soon as she was able, Tricia turned on Paul, her brain whirling with questions. She couldn't help but wonder what information he'd left out when telling them of his background. If an innocent touch on his arm could startle him to the point of doing violence, what kind of people had he associated with before coming here? "Why on earth would you overreact like that?" she demanded. "Are you crazy? A normal person wouldn't practically assault someone for trying to wake them up. This isn't a war zone for crying out loud!"

"I said I was sorry," Paul said sheepishly, his mind working feverishly to think up a plausible excuse for his behavior. He could hardly tell her that his overly zealous response was due to his profession, where a man caught unaware could easily turn up dead. As angry as Tricia was with him, he was far more angry with himself for demonstrating such paranoia. He couldn't remember the last time he'd slept so soundly, but he didn't have time to explore the cause.

Aurie and Patricia Courteau were looking at him with the kind of curiosity he couldn't afford, not if he didn't want this charade to come to an untimely end. From now on, he couldn't let his guard down for a single second, not even when he was asleep. "I must have been having some kind of a weird dream," he said, wishing he could have come up with a more convincing explanation.

"Sounds more like a nightmare to me," Aurie pronounced sympathetically.

One down, one to go, Paul judged silently, then turned to the more skeptical female of the twosome. "I can't remember the exact details, but I think I was being attacked by a huge herd of Chester Whites and it was either defend myself or get trampled underhoof."

Upon hearing that, Tricia decided it would be prudent on her part to leave well enough alone and get on to other matters. The last thing she wanted was for Paul to launch into a detailed description of this morning's misadventure in the barn. That would only add more fuel to the matchmaking fire Grannie hoped to light under them. "Well, now that you're awake, I'd like to discuss some changes that are going to take place here starting tomorrow."

"Changes?" Aurie queried suspiciously, squinting through her glasses at Tricia who had reclaimed her chair and suggested that Paul do the same. "What kind of changes and who's making 'em?"

"We all are," Tricia declared firmly, determined to make a stand. Brown eyes locked with Aurie's hazel ones, she reminded, "Grannie, you've known all along that I came back here to start up my own business and I'm not waiting any longer to begin. I know you were hoping that I'd keep putting it off, but the ladies' craft and sewing circle meets tomorrow night and I'm going to that meeting."

"What if we have a late farrowing tomorrow? Old number eleven is due any day now," Aurie put in, but not with her usual spirit. Although Tricia rarely exhibited the trait, Aurie knew that her granddaughter's stubborn streak ran as deeply as her own. "That sow always has trouble giving birth."

"Our hired man will be there to handle it," Tricia decided, ignoring Paul's horrified expression. "I'll tell him what needs to be done if Betty Sue goes into labor. Anybody can clip, tie and shear and Paul has the advantage of having been raised on a farm."

"Now wait a minute." Paul's fearful gulp was audible. "We didn't own any pigs. Clip, tie and shear what?"

Sensing a possibly ally, Aurie couldn't wait to tell him. "Once the litter's born, you gotta clip and tie the navel cord of each pig. Then you take a pair of clippers and shear off their needle teeth so they can't grow into tusks. You also gotta' notch their ears and give 'em their shots."

"Tricia," Paul began a bit desperately. "I don't know if I'm capable..."

"Didn't you tell me you came here to find out whether or not you're cut out for this kind of work?"

"Yes, but..."

"Make no buts about it. You're not going to last two minutes on your own place if you back down at the first little challenge," Tricia charged. "The birth

process is a never-ending thing on any successful farm.
Or weren't you planning on raising stock?''

Recalling his plans, Paul had to admit that they'd
not only been slightly nebulous, but also a bit on the
idealistic side. More and more often over the last
twenty years, he'd associated the grim realities of life
with his work in law enforcement, comforting himself with what he could now see were pretty sopho-
moric dreams of one day retiring to a world of pastoral
bliss.

In the last twenty-four hours, Tricia had managed
to poke several holes in that particular fantasy and he
greatly feared that before she got through with him,
she was going to poke quite a few more. "I plan to
raise stock, but not necessarily pigs," he finally admitted with a nervous shrug. "I was thinking I'd buy
a couple of cows and some horses. Maybe a few
chickens."

"Hah! You won't make no kind of a living thinking that small," Aurie expounded, inadvertently
placing herself on Tricia's side of the debate. "Now-
adays you've got to be specialized and you've got to do
it up big if you 'spect to make any money farming. I
know a few things about cows and horses and chickens and I can tell you, pigs are a darn sight better than
any of 'em. Name me one other animal that converts
thirty-five percent of what he eats to meat? Cows and
sheep don't do more than eleven and horses ain't good
for much of anything but show."

As her grandmother lambasted a harassed-looking
Paul with a harrowing tale about her experience with
what she called "them persnickety, pantywaist poul-
try," Tricia searched her mind for an effective way of
regaining control of the conversation and redirecting

it onto the path she wanted it to take. Unfortunately, when Grannie was on a roll, nothing and no one could stop her. All Tricia could do was sit back and wait for an opening.

That opportunity came a few moments later when Paul threw up his hands and said, "I swear, Mrs. Courteau, before I decide one way or the other, I'll give hog husbandry every consideration."

"Starting first thing in the morning," Tricia invited hopefully.

Paul was so anxious to escape another lecture, he would have agreed to anything. "Starting right now if you want."

Tricia fought down the urge to laugh. "That won't be necessary," she assured him, and quickly relayed her future intentions while she had the chance. "The routine we followed this morning doesn't change much from day to day until spring. When I'm not busy, I'll be here to help out with chores, but they can be handled by one person. I've been doing it by myself for the last two weeks."

She glanced over at Aurie to make sure she was paying attention. "Now that we've got a hired man again, I should be able to take some days off to build up my contacts. Then, as soon as Paul really gets the hang of things around here, I'll be free to devote the majority of my time to my business. That *is* what we're paying him for."

With a pointed lift of her brows, she inquired, "Isn't that right, Grannie?"

"We're not paying him much," Aurie said.

"Considering his admitted inexperience, what we're paying him is more than fair. Wouldn't you say so, Paul?"

"It's fair," he acknowledged, unaware of the going rate, and unwilling to cast even more suspicion on his already questionable qualifications for employment by taking issue with his salary.

Satisfied with the response from that quarter, Tricia turned back to her grandmother. "And having your support while I start up my own business was the idea when I agreed to move in with you, wasn't it, Grannie?"

Aurie gave a grudging nod and looked at Paul, obviously hoping he'd offer further resistance since she couldn't without looking as if she'd gone back on her word. Like her, Paul didn't have a high regard for the way things were shaping up, but short of quitting, what could he do about it? Tricia had them both over a barrel and she knew it.

Tasting victory, Tricia continued, "Don't look so worried, Paul. Tomorrow I'll show you how to operate the automatic drinking fountains and how to mix feed. It's really not that hard. If Betty Sue goes into labor while I'm gone, I'll show you how to set up the metal guardrails that will keep her from rolling over on her babies and everything else you'll need to know to help care for her young. All right?"

"I guess so," Paul replied uncertainly.

Expelling a deep breath, Tricia clasped her hands together and smiled. "This is going to work out great."

"Great," Paul muttered gloomily.

"Now that we've got that all settled, I think I'll go to bed," Tricia announced as she stood up from her chair and headed for the front stairs. She was on the third step before she remembered another subject she'd neglected to bring up.

Keeping one hand on the carved walnut handrail, she turned her head and looked back over her shoulder. "I forgot to mention one other change I'd like to make. From now on, Paul, I'd appreciate your help with the supper dishes. As far as I know, we both put in the same hours today so I don't see why I should do all the clean-up chores by myself."

"Patricia Louise!" Aurie exclaimed, shocked by her granddaughter's unheard-of request. "You can't ask a man to come in and wash dirty dishes after a long, hard day's work. Why, my Howard never lifted a finger in the kitchen and neither did your father and I never expected them to."

"Well, I expect this one to," Tricia stated firmly, more determined than ever to get her way when she saw the thumbs-up signal Paul tossed at Aurie to urge her on.

Aurie was aghast at Tricia's militant stand. The girl might never find a husband if this was how she treated a good, hardworking man. "Now, Tricia, Amos has been working here for more than twenty years and we've never expected him to clean up after meals."

"Amos doesn't eat his evening meal with us," Tricia reminded her evenly. "Paul does. So, if I'm expected to come in and wash dishes after a long, hard day's work, so can he."

"Well, I never!" Aurie declared, realizing that her granddaughter wasn't going to budge on this issue. "If you're so all-fired, put out over this, Tricia, I'll do the supper dishes myself, just like I used to."

Tricia threw Paul a killing glance. "That won't be necessary, will it, Paul?"

"I don't mind helping," Paul inserted quickly, realizing that Tricia might be the one who was all fired

up, but he'd be the one who would be put out if he
didn't come to her aid. "As Tricia says, it's only fair
and I agree with her."

"Well, I never!" Aurie repeated, shaking her head
in bemusement as Tricia gave Paul the thumbs-up signal, then turned around and continued on up the
stairs.

Two weeks later, Paul had good reason to regret his
compliance with Tricia's ideas on sexual equality and
the equal division of labor. He was standing before the
kitchen sink, up to his elbows in dirty dishwater while
she was about to dash out the door on her way to visit
some local craftswomen. If he didn't know how excited she was over the progress she'd made with her
business in so short a time, he would've stated his
grievance. He'd been stuck doing all the dishes for the
last three nights in a row. As it was, not only hadn't he
complained, but he'd also volunteered for the job so
she could follow through on the promising contacts
she'd established at the ladies' circle meeting.

Studying her as she drew on her coat, Paul was curious as to why she'd gotten so dressed up. Normally,
she went out in slacks and a sweater, but tonight she
was wearing a royal blue suede dress that lovingly
draped the slender curves of her body. Her legs were
encased in shimmery textured hose, the sexiness enhanced by three-inch heels.

He was grateful that she'd put on her coat for the
slit he noticed at the side of her clingy skirt was giving
him some very unacceptable ideas and he didn't want
to ruin what he'd worked so hard for two agonizingly
long weeks to achieve. Since that episode in the truck
when he'd almost lost control, he'd done an excellent
job of keeping his distance from her. Getting Tricia to

feel at ease in his presence had taken a tremendous toll on his bodily well-being, but somehow he'd managed it.

Just this morning, Tricia had complimented him on how quickly he'd mastered the skills required of him as their hired hand and how well she thought they were working together. It was a lucky thing she hadn't looked like this during chores or she wouldn't be applauding his work skills, but his talents in an entirely different area.

"Who's on the agenda tonight, good lookin'?" he inquired, in what he hoped was a brotherly tone.

Hands in her pockets, Tricia opened her brown leather coat and twirled around like a high fashion model, showing off the sarong-style skirt and high mandarin collar of her favorite dress. "I am looking good," she claimed gaily. "And I'm going to knock the socks off of Larry I've-got-the-connections Wheeler."

Before Paul could ask who this Wheeler guy was, Aurie came into the kitchen and took her usual place in her rocker near the stove. "Hmmph! If you'd married that boy when he asked you, you wouldn't have to go beggin' to him now. He sure would've been a darned sight better than that Mangioni person."

"I'm not going begging, Grannie," Tricia replied, in such high spirits that she wasn't the least exasperated with Aurie's pithy comments. Nor did she see Paul stiffen at the name of her ex-fiancé.

Aurie did. Unaware of his professional interest in her granddaughter's relationship with Joseph Mangioni, she decided that Paul was jealous. She wasn't above using that emotion to provoke a ripple in what she felt were some disappointingly calm waters. "That young man has carried a torch for you ever since high school. Larry's a rich man now, Tricia. If you give him a chance, he just might propose again."

Aurie didn't miss the quick glance Tricia shot at Paul before she said, "Someday, maybe, but tonight we're going to discuss the possibility of my leasing a booth at the country craft fair in Chicago. It's the biggest event of its kind in the country and booths are booked up months in advance, but Larry thinks he might still be able to get me in. I'll only have two weeks to get my act together, but I want to try. Larry says if people show enough interest in what I'm trying to sell, he just might consider renting me some space at River Run. Dear old Larry, he always was a good friend."

"What and where is a river run?" Paul inquired, forgetting all the questions he'd like to ask her about her past relationship with Joseph Mangioni as he considered her current association with "dear old Larry." First off, he wanted to know just how old and dear a man was he? Secondly, exactly what did she mean by good friend?

"River Run is one of the biggest tourist traps on the Mississippi," Aurie spat.

"One of the better ones," Tricia disagreed. "River Run is like a reconstruction of a nineteenth century village. Besides an old country inn, it's got a general store and lots of different specialty stores. It would be the perfect place for me to open my consignment shop."

Tricia might have said more but the mantel clock chimed the hour and she realized that she was running late. "I'm supposed to meet Larry at seven-thirty. I've really got to run," she apologized as she scooped up her purse off the kitchen table and hurried to the door. Her hand was on the knob before she remembered her manners. "Thanks for doing the dishes, Paul. I'll make it up to you, I promise."

Wrestling with an unexpected and very primitive emotion, Paul turned to look at her and saw out of the corner of his eye that Aurie was on her way back to the living room. If he had anything to say about it, this Larry guy was going to wait a while longer. He spoke to Tricia in a low, husky drawl, letting his possessive gaze drift slowly down her body. "Lady, I'm going to hold you to that promise."

Since Paul had displayed no sexually aggressive moves since that first day, Tricia couldn't have been more astonished. As many times as she'd told herself that she was glad he'd changed his mind about wanting her, there'd been other times when she'd ached so badly for his touch that she'd felt like starting something. Caught off guard by this sudden switch in his behavior, she didn't know what she wanted and her confusion showed in her expression. "Yes...well...I guess that means I get to do dishes for the rest of the week."

"Not necessarily," Paul murmured, holding her gaze.

Tricia could almost hear the wild suggestion he was making with his vivid gray eyes and it was so compelling and electric that she swayed toward him, her heart pounding in an erratic rhythm. She steadied herself by holding onto the doorknob as if it were a lifeline. If he could wield this kind of power over her merely through the use of his eyes, what would she do if he brought more of his considerably potent weapons into play?

She gulped down a surge of sheer panic and brought up another man's name, using it like a smoke screen to hide behind. "I don't want to keep Larry waiting so I'd better get going."

"Patience is a virtue," Paul advised silkily. "Waiting is one of the things I do best." He lowered his voice and when he spoke again, Tricia felt as if each word was a searing, hot caress. "Of course, there are a number of other things I do even better."

"I'm sure there are," Tricia croaked, knowing exactly what those other things were.

"If you weren't in such a hurry, I could demonstrate one or two of them for you now," he suggested huskily.

"Sorry, I'm flat out of time." Tricia wrenched open the door, practically falling onto the back porch in her haste to leave the house. Paul's chuckle accompanied her flight and his warning, "Don't be sorry. I'll still be here when you get home," followed her all the way to the River Run Lounge where she was meeting Larry Wheeler for a drink.

By the end of the evening, she'd had several.

Six

Aurie retired to her first floor bedroom, right on schedule at 8:00 p.m. and nothing short of an earthquake would wake her. With Tricia out for the evening, Paul could check in at the bureau by nine without fear of discovery. When Tricia was around, he had to be far more secretive about his activities, so from that standpoint, her absence made his job that much easier. He'd accomplished quite a lot in the last hour. He'd even managed an in-depth search of her room, something he'd avoided doing since his arrival. Professionally speaking, he was making some progress.

Looked at from another angle, however—a strictly personal one—he didn't like searching Tricia's room, invading her privacy, asking personal questions about her that were none of his business. She was just beginning to trust him, to like him, and he betrayed that

liking and trust whenever she turned her back. She
might be the one suspected of a crime, but he was the
one who felt like a criminal.

No choice, he reminded himself as he walked into
his own bedroom and locked the door behind him. *If
you want to prove her innocent, you've got no choice.*
Sitting down on the bed, he reached for the pad of
paper on the nightstand and studied the name he was
about to pass on to the bureau—Lawrence Wheeler,
dear old Larry, handsome, rich, torchbearing Larry
who even now might be cozying up to his old high
school flame.

With a violent motion of his wrist, Paul ripped the
page off the pad and placed it in the center of a large
ashtray. Gray eyes glinting, he lit a match and watched
the paper burn until the man's name disintegrated into
nothing. He glanced at his watch, confirming for the
hundredth time that Tricia had only been gone a couple of hours. Every minute of that time had seemed
like an eternity and his imagination was working
overtime wondering what she was doing. He knew
what he'd have been doing if he was out with her.

He swore with quiet vengeance, then released some
more of his pent-up hostility on the push-button
phone, wishing he could picture a particular man's
dear old face as he punched out the special code number.

Sam Mitchell came on the line and was immediately aware of the disgruntled edge in Paul's voice.
"Can I gather by that surly greeting that nothing's
changed from the last time you called? You're still
positive that the Courteau broad is innocent but you
still don't have any proof, right?"

Disliking the chief's reference to Tricia as a "broad," Paul closed his eyes as the truth hit him. He could deny it for all he was worth, but it was no use. He had it bad, really bad, and if he wasn't careful Mitchell was going to have him pulled off this case. "Mangioni was mentioned tonight," he stated calmly. "I got the chance to question the grandmother who I consider a pretty good judge of character. She didn't know anything about Mangioni's criminal connections and she still despises the guy. The more I find out about it, the more certain I am that Patricia didn't know anything either. The engagement was pretty short-lived."

Reluctantly, he backed up that premise with the results of his search. "It's all here in her diary, Mitchell," he said, feeling like a heel for betraying the personal information he'd found between the tear-stained pages of a leather-bound book. "She was an eighteen-year-old, gullible virgin, away from home for the first time, and she fell for an age-old line. The guy wanted her body and promised her marriage to get it. There's nothing here to suggest she ever saw him again after that."

Sam reacted to the information as expected. "I'll make sure the diary is listed if we call for a warrant."

Jaw clenched, Paul inquired, "What about our other suspects? Has anyone come up with anything useful?"

"Nope. Your woman still heads the list, Lansing. That sample you sent for chemical analysis matches up. It's the same drug."

Paul tried not to sound defensive as he reminded, "Easy access isn't proof of anything, and you know it."

"So far, it's better than anything else we've got," Mitchell responded.

Paul let that pass. "Check out the name Lawrence Wheeler for me, will you? He owns a place called River Run, a local tourist stop. Patricia is out with him tonight trying to make arrangements to get a booth at some country craft fair in Chicago. Evidently, the guy plans to pull a few strings so she can get space there to exhibit. And while you're at it, you might as well check out this fair. It's scheduled to take place in a couple of weeks."

"When exactly?" Sam Mitchell asked, his tone conveying far more interest than the information should have inspired.

"I don't have the exact dates."

"Get 'em!" Mitchell ordered and Paul felt a sickening lurch in the pit of his stomach. He heard a shuffle of papers and then the chief's voice came back on the line. "Never mind, I've got them right here."

"Since when do you keep a list of things like that?" Paul wanted to know.

Sam proceeded to tell him about the government case going before the Grand Jury during the last week in March. "If nothing happens to our witnesses, we've got a good chance for conviction, Lansing. Since you're telling me that our chief suspect plans to be in town at the same time, I can't help but think that she's arranging for her next hit. This country craft fair thing is going on within a block of the court house."

"It's got to be another coincidence," Paul muttered grimly, frustrated with the number of casual relationships that kept cropping up to prevent his proving Tricia's innocence. He knew in his gut that she wasn't capable of murder, yet the evidence against her

kept mounting. All he could do to save her was to
continue doing his job in the best way he knew how
and pray that the real guilty party would soon be
found out.

"Okay, Mitchell," Paul continued. "Check out this
Wheeler guy for me and I'll arrange for a phone tap on
this line. If Tricia goes to Chicago, I'll make sure I'm
right there with her. In the meantime, I suggest you
advise our other operatives to keep a close eye on their
subjects. I swear to you, Sam, every instinct I've got
says that Patricia Courteau isn't our lady and they've
never led me wrong before."

"Maybe this time your instincts have gotten side-
tracked by a beautiful woman," Sam Mitchell suggested quietly, no longer speaking as Paul's boss but
as his friend. "You've got to remember who we're
dealing with here, Paul. The 'Scarlet Lady' makes men
go willingly to their deaths. Her victims all died with
a smile on their faces, but they were still just as dead.
It sounds to me like your Patricia has the same seduc-
tive talent. Don't let her play you for a fool, pal."

"She's not playing me for anything and she's not
my Patricia," Paul objected harshly even though deep
down in his heart he'd already accepted that he wanted
her to be his in every way possible. In the next instant, he was struck by an unthinkable notion. What
if he took the "lady" to bed himself? Then, he'd know
first hand if she had the sexual skills necessary to make
so many men die happy. Right or wrong, he'd know.

"Be careful, Paul," Sam Mitchell warned as if he'd
been able to hear Paul's thoughts. "Be very careful
how you handle her."

"Don't worry, Chief," Paul asserted flatly. "Nothing I do will jeopardize our investigation. I want the

'Scarlet Lady' brought to justice even more than you do.''

Mitchell sighed. "If it turns out you're right and the Courteau woman isn't our gal, I've lost you as an agent, haven't I?''

Paul didn't say anything as several different images streaked across his mind. Tricia, down on her knees on a braided rag rug, playing with a fat, brown puppy. Grannie Aurie shaking a finger under his nose and demanding that he wear warmer socks so he wouldn't catch cold. He and Tricia working side by side in the barn. The steady ticking of the mantel clock in the living room as all three of them sat before a warm fire and argued over who would get what section of the evening paper first.

So many images. So many warm wonderful feelings he'd never felt before. "I don't know, Sam," he finally admitted honestly. "I'm finding lots of answers here, yet each one leads me to a new question. But whatever happens, I need to thank you for giving me this assignment. It's given me a better perspective on a number of things . . . and people that I've put off thinking about for too long.''

"You're a damned good agent, Lancelot," Sam declared stoutly. "Think about that while you're at it.''

"Yes, I am," Paul agreed without conceit. "And until this case is solved one way or another, that's all I am.''

Their conversation was concluded very shortly thereafter. After hanging up the phone, Paul picked up Tricia's diary off the bed and returned it to the middle drawer of the antique oak writing desk in her room. As soon as that task was done, his frame of mind changed from that of a government agent to that of a man. No matter what he'd recently told his chief, there was no way he could prevent himself from being a man with a man's needs.

As such, he experienced a typically human response to being inside the room of the woman he desired so intensely at times that he thought he'd go crazy. He was curious about everything in it, from the white iron single bed with its crocheted lace coverlet to the collection of hand-painted porcelain figures standing behind the glass doors of the antique curio cabinet. Each item in the room matched some facet of its feminine owner's personality.

Tricia's interest in country crafts was apparent in the handmade quilt folded up on the end of her bed, in the stitched, crewelwork pictures hanging beneath the rose-patterned stencils on the walls and in the quaint, hand-painted gnomestone village set atop her highboy bureau. Her love of travel was brought home in a mounted collection of fragrant, beribboned sachets, each proclaiming the name of the country of purchase. Her bookshelf contained works of poetry, a few classics, several historical romances, a stack of Sears catalogs and one or two animal husbandry textbooks.

It was a lovely, feminine room done up in creamy beiges that reminded Paul of Tricia's lovely skin and soft shades of rose that reminded him of her sweet feminine lips. It was a room that cried out for the presence of a man to balance its delicacy with strength, its female vivacity with male virility. As he sat down on the dainty, pristine coverlet of her single bed, Paul was more determined than ever to be the one who would answer that call.

* * *

It was after midnight when Tricia and Larry finished reminiscing over old times. Back in high school, they'd both run around with the same gang of kids. Tricia had lost touch with most of them since moving to Minneapolis, but Larry had stayed in the area and still knew everyone's whereabouts. All in all, they'd spent an enjoyable evening, especially when Larry had relayed the news that he'd managed to wangle Tricia a space at the upcoming fair.

As luck would have it, Larry Wheeler and Darryl Barnes, one of the fair's organizers, had attended Drake University together. When Tricia had made a wistful mention of Chicago's annual country craft show, Larry had known immediately that he could get her in. During their four years in the fraternity house, Darryl had accumulated quite a debt to his smart, handsome frat brother Larry. According to Larry, poor Darryl would have never had a date if Larry hadn't intervened on his behalf and would've flunked out of half his classes.

If she ever met the man, Tricia prayed she wouldn't slip up and call him "Daft Darryl" as Larry did. Unlike his fraternity buddy, she owed the man her eternal gratitude. Due to his generosity in allotting space for her at this late date, her consignment business would be off to a great start.

Because of the amount of alcohol she'd consumed throughout the evening, Tricia was feeling more than a little tipsy when Larry escorted her out to her car. If she hadn't been, she never would have allowed him to kiss her good-night. They'd enjoyed a brief, high school infatuation that had fizzled out as quickly as it had begun. The last thing she wanted to do was stir up any old embers.

Larry Wheeler was tall, blond and good-looking. He was intelligent and had a great personality. A successful businessman, he was every grandmother's idea of a perfect catch, but as far as Tricia was concerned, their romance was long since dead and would stay that way.

Apparently, Larry wasn't as sure as she was that they'd never be more than friends. "I'd like us to start seeing each other again, Tricia," he said, staring affectionately down into her slightly glazed-looking brown eyes. "I had a great time tonight talking over old times."

"It was fun," Tricia agreed, leaning back against her car to keep from falling down. She'd hoped that the cold night air would clear her head but it seemed to be having the opposite effect. Finding the right words was becoming more and more difficult each passing second. "I'm sorry, Larry, but it wouldn't be a good idea for us to go out again."

A tiny hiccup preceded her next slurred admission, "You see, I've got this really...drop-dead hunk of a man at home so I can only think of you as a friend."

She passed a hand over her eyes and frowned at her blurred vision. Considering the twenty-mile return trip to the farm, this was not good. "Unfortunately, he also drives me to drink and that's why I'm in this unfortunate condition. Under the circumstances, I really hate to ask you this, Larry, but would you mind taking me home?"

It was proof of his friendship that the man didn't even hesitate. After assisting Tricia into the passenger side of her car, he walked around and slid behind the wheel. Once they were on the road, he said, "I'll leave your car near the inn and you can come back and pick it up tomorrow. The keys will be under the seat."

"You're a nice man, Larry," Tricia complimented sleepily.

"But not a drop-dead hunk," he reminded wryly, lips twitching as he noted Tricia's valiant struggle to stay awake. "You can use my lap for a pillow if you want to. Nice men don't carry tales to hunks. That's why we live long and prosper."

The man who was gazing out a second-story window when Tricia's car pulled into the drive was moved to disprove that theory as soon as he saw her straighten up from her reclining position in the front seat. A burst of white-hot jealousy curled his hands into fists and brought a surge of adrenaline to his legs. He was down the stairs in ten seconds flat and flinging open the front door before the couple outside had reached the threshold.

"That's him," Tricia announced glumly as Larry guided her drunken progress toward the house.

Larry was hard put to keep from laughing when the furious-looking man on the other side of the door wrenched Tricia away from him as soon as they were inside. "Didn't I tell you?" she declared petulantly, but Larry noticed that she made no effort to escape the steely arm wrapped around her waist.

"She's drunk!" Paul bit out angrily, sounding very much like an irate parent.

Larry decided against offering his hand and introducing himself. With one glimpse at the competition, he'd removed himself from the race. It was obvious to him that he was way out of this man's league. From what he'd seen thus far, he feared that Tricia was playing a little out of her league too. Maybe he could help her out by leaving her hunk with a little food for thought. "If you don't want her coming home like this, fella, then don't drive her to drink. She deserves better treatment."

"What!"

"You heard me," Larry charged bravely. "I said treat her right and you won't have this problem."

Paul committed Wheeler's face to memory in case he was forced to hunt him down at a later date. If he didn't have a thoroughly inebriated female on his hands, later would have been now. "You want to explain that remark to me, buddy?"

Larry shrugged and turned up the collar of his overcoat. "Ask Tricia." That said, he swiveled on his heel and marched back outside.

"You bet I will," Paul swore vehemently as he kicked the door shut with his bare foot and the pain shot all the way up his leg.

Tricia rallied slightly when Paul swung her off the floor and into his arms, but he'd mounted only two steps before she gave up the effort and relaxed in his arms. Luxuriating in the warmth and strength of the muscular chest beneath her cheek, that unique masculine smell of his that never failed to please her, she snuggled against him like a cuddly, contented kitten. "You smell so good," she whispered. "Just like you taste."

Paul tried to calm down, but her words enraged him all over again. He'd caught a whiff of Wheeler's expensive cologne, but smelling was one thing and tasting quite another. "You like his taste, honey?" he challenged her darkly. "Well, you're going to love mine!"

Bypassing her room, Paul stalked down the hallway into his. He pulled down the quilt, then lowered Tricia on to the sheets, gray eyes never leaving hers as he stripped off his clothes. When he was naked, he sat down on the mattress beside her and started in on her coat.

"Are you going to make love to me now?" she inquired curiously, doing nothing to help him remove her clothes, but not resisting either.

"Yes, I am," Paul confirmed as he stripped off her dress, then her panty hose and slip and finally her lace bra and panties. He looked down at the length of her slender body with something like awe, but then his nostrils flared. "By morning, you'll realize that I'm the only man you want touching you. I'm going to make love to you until you can't think of anyone else but me."

"Okay," Tricia mumbled happily, beamed him a smile and promptly passed out.

Paul stared at her limp form for several seconds before he accepted the inevitable. "Damn you, woman," he cursed on a long, deflated breath as he slid beneath the sheets. "How could you do this to me?"

Tricia opened her eyes, blinked once and closed them again. The digital clock on the nightstand said it was 3:00 a.m., not yet time to wake up. But she couldn't fall back asleep. The delicious sensations singing through her body were what had awakened her in the first place and rather than abating, they were growing stronger.

Murmuring softly, she arched her back and the hand that tenderly caressed her right breast increased its stroking. She moaned with the pleasure and turned toward the warmth that enveloped her from behind. Smiling, she pressed her breasts against Paul's naked chest, entwining her legs with his as she reveled in the realistic nature of her dream. Then, as his mouth closed over her waiting nipple, she opened her eyes and realized that the sensations she was feeling seemed so realistic because they weren't being provoked by a loving figment of her imagination but by the man himself.

Paul Lansing in the flesh—warm, hard, naked flesh!

With a shocked squeak, Tricia pushed him away and sat up in the bed. "What's going on here?" she demanded, cheeks flaming as she realized that she was just as naked as he. "What are you doing in my room?"

"Loving you," he explained simply, surveying the rosy flush that covered her body with knowing gray eyes. "But this is my room, sleepyhead, not yours."

Clutching a sheet over her bare breasts, Tricia's eyes went very wide. Had she been so drunk when she'd come in tonight that she'd somehow wandered into his bed? Or even worse, had the alcohol lowered her inhibitions to the point that she'd actually invited this to happen? "I . . . I don't remember anything."

Since Paul had spent the last two hours watching her sleep, she wasn't telling him anything he didn't already know. He pushed himself up on his elbows and said, "That's because you passed out as soon as we came in here, which leads me to the question I've been wanting to ask you ever since. What do you mean telling that Wheeler guy that I drove you to drink?"

"Oh, no," Tricia groaned, as partial memory returned. She had said that and a few other damning things as well. She'd told Larry that she couldn't get involved with him because she already had a man at home. What if he went around telling people that she was having an affair with her hired man? If a rumor like that ever got back to Grannie, there'd be hell to pay. "Me and my big mouth. This is awful, just awful!"

Paul didn't know if she was passing judgment on her current position in his bed or something that had transpired during the evening, but he meant to find out. She sounded on the verge of panic. "What's so awful?"

Since Paul would suffer for her thoughtless choice of words just as much as she would if they ever got back to Grannie, Tricia felt she had no choice but to tell him what she'd done. And the fact that they were naked together in bed wasn't going to make it any easier. If she hadn't come to her senses in time, right now they'd be doing exactly what Larry Wheeler thought they'd been doing for who knows how long.

Paul studied her stricken expression and repeated his first question. "Why would that guy tell me to start treating you better, Tricia? What's going on?"

"Well...um...Larry got the impression that you and I aren't getting along very well."

"Why would you give him an impression like that?" Paul asked stiffly. "We've been getting along just fine and you know it."

"It's kind of hard to explain. I didn't actually say we had a fight. Larry just thought that was what I meant."

Goaded by the gray eyes boring relentlessly into her face, Tricia burst out, "It's all your fault, Paul Lansing! If you hadn't gotten me all hot and bothered before I went out tonight, I wouldn't have drunk so much and then I wouldn't have said what I did to Larry."

"So I got you all hot and bothered, did I?" Paul inquired with a wide grin, not even trying to hide his satisfaction.

"Yes, you did," Tricia admitted resentfully.

"So what else did you say to the man that you shouldn't have said?" Paul asked, obviously looking forward to her answer.

The rosy flush on Tricia's cheeks flamed hotter. "I kind of implied... Well, Larry thinks that we're...sort of intimately involved."

Tricia gasped when Paul grabbed the sheet out of her clenched hands and cast it aside. An instant later, she found herself beneath him, aware of him with every fiber of her being. Her heart went wild and her body throbbed in pleasure.

"I kinda, sorta think we are, too," Paul murmured huskily, feeling her instant response. "Don't you?"

"Paul...no...we shouldn't...we can't do this," Tricia moaned as his thigh moved between hers and his mouth began to string slow, languorous kisses over her breasts.

"Yes, we can," Paul assured her thickly. "We have to, Tricia. We've waited long enough as it is."

Desire surged through her with each touch of his lips and even as she told herself that she shouldn't surrender, her legs twined instinctively with his. "You...you don't understand what will happen.... Oh!" She sucked in her breath as his lips closed around one nipple.

"I don't care what happens," Paul muttered hoarsely, then used his tongue to further incite the anticipation he felt in her body. "I want you, Tricia. Feel how much I want you."

A strange sensation of feminine power sprang to life inside her and Tricia gave in to the need that had been plaguing her ever since this man had first entered her life. She lifted her arms to circle his neck and his mouth was there, waiting to receive her parted lips. Her fingers fluttered down the contours of his back and then began to blindly clutch at him as her passion rose higher.

Paul wanted her. With his mouth, hands and body he wanted her, almost as much as her mouth, hands and body wanted him. Tricia kissed him, clung to him, moved with him. Her nails were gripping his shoulders ruthlessly and he groaned in response, urging her to even more primitive actions.

The soft moans that came from far back in her throat were elemental cries of need and Paul reacted to them fiercely. His hands dug into her buttocks, making her gasp, then his fingers trailed around to the soft, heated place between her legs and Tricia reacted with helpless abandon.

"That's it, sweetheart," he encouraged. "Give me that fire. I need to feel it all burning for me."

"Please, Paul!" Tricia lifted her hips and he increased the tempo of his caresses, letting her feel the strength of his manhood against her thigh. "I need you too, so very much."

Her soft pleas captured him as no woman's ever had and he thrust inside her, glorying in the feel of her surrounding him. His head spun as he established a rhythm to match the wondrously female ebb and flow that possessed her. In none of the dreams of her had she opened herself so completely, burned for him so beautifully. As long as he lived, he'd never forget it.

Tricia felt herself filled, her body stretched deliciously tight until each nerve ending threatened to explode. Up and up the heavy, thrusting rhythm went, driving her to a place where reality no longer existed. It was a dazzling place of timeless emotions and perpetual pleasure that could only be occupied by the two of them and they were each just as desperate to reach it.

Then they were both crying out each other's names as the pulsing completion spun them away to their ultimate destination and even if they'd tried, there was no turning back.

Paul recovered slowly. It took him several moments to grasp that the woman under him was no longer panting with excitement but taking long calming breaths. He was trying his best to control his own breathing. He found himself gazing down into the bottomless depths of her soft brown eyes, and he couldn't begin to read the mixture of emotions swirling there.

He whispered her name as he reluctantly unsealed their bodies. "Are you all right?" He settled down beside her, cradling her in the crook of his arm.

"Yes." She closed her eyes on a troubled sigh.

He'd felt the total response of her body, heard the words of desire on her lips, so why the anxious sigh? He knew he'd made her feel things she'd never felt before, so why was she closing him out? He could sense her mental desertion, but after what they'd just shared he refused to stand for it. "This was right, Tricia. Tell me you know that's true, that you don't regret what's happened."

"It's too late for regrets," Tricia whispered in a shattered tone. She opened her eyes and shook her head. "Oh, Paul, we've really done it now."

Seven

——

"What have we done?" Paul sat up in bed and pulled Tricia up to face him. "We made love, beautiful, incredible love, that's what. Now you tell me what you think is so wrong with that."

Tricia heard the suppressed anger, and, unbelievably, the genuine hurt in Paul's tone and rushed to correct his misinterpretation. She couldn't stand for him to think that she hadn't loved every second of their loving. "I don't think there's anything wrong with what we did. It was an incredible experience. How we feel about it isn't the problem, Paul. It's how other people will feel that is going to make things difficult for us."

"Other people?" Paul shook his head in confusion. "What other people? Unless you're aware of something I'm not, we're all alone in this room. Nobody else knows what we've been doing so what the devil are you so worried about?''

"This is a small town, Paul." Tricia ignored his mocking tone. "Knowing Larry, news of our relationship will get around fast and there'll be all kinds of wild conjectures made about us. You don't know what people are like around here. If they think we're having an illicit love affair, Grannie won't be able to hold her head up in society and I can kiss my business good-bye."

"Illicit love affair!" Paul expounded incredulously. "For God's sake, Tricia, this might be a small town, but this isn't the middle ages. Neither of us is married, we're both consenting adults and as far as I know, what we just did isn't against the law."

"Maybe not any civil law, but that won't prevent people from making moral judgments against us," Tricia insisted, trying desperately to make him understand. "The only way they'd turn a blind eye to this kind of behavior is if they thought we were engaged. I know it's hard to believe in this day and age, but that's really the way things are around here."

Paul threw up his hands in defeat. "So if anyone asks, we'll tell them we're engaged."

For an instant, Tricia wondered if she'd just received some kind of a proposal and she felt a brief shaft of joy in the region of her heart. Then she understood what Paul was actually proposing and a surge of anger overrode all other feelings. "I'm sure you'd like that just fine," she declared tartly. "But I have no intention of compounding one lie with an even bigger one. I'm not going to deceive my friends and family just so I can go on sleeping with you."

Without stopping to think, Paul retorted, "Who says we'd be lying?"

Tricia's mouth dropped open. "Are you ... are you saying you actually want to marry me?"

Paul almost swallowed his own Adam's apple as he realized that was exactly what he was saying. What's more, he highly resented her doubting his integrity. If she knew the reasons why he'd showed up on her farm, she'd have good reason to doubt it, but she didn't know, and if things worked out right, he wouldn't have to tell her until he was sure that she'd forgive him.

If a woman loved a man in any way that counted, she'd have to forgive him, wouldn't she? After tonight, Paul planned to do his level best to make Tricia love him in all the countless ways he'd just accepted that he loved her.

If her passionate response to his lovemaking was any indication, she was more than halfway there already. No woman could have given herself so completely to a man without feeling some very intense emotion. Of course, he hadn't planned to declare himself until he'd cleared her name of all suspicion at the bureau, but then Larry Wheeler had arrived on the scene and he'd lost his head. Now it was too late for them to go back to the way things had been. He'd made her his and he wouldn't allow her to deny it to herself, to him or to anyone else.

"You can't be serious," Tricia scoffed when the silence became unbearable.

"I'm very serious," Paul replied with fierce male conviction. If she thought to keep him at arm's length with the puritanical notions of a bunch of small-minded people, she didn't know him very well.

"But we barely know each other!" Tricia blurted, confirming Paul's last thought.

Tricia's fearful plea earned her a flash of dimples and a searing gaze. "I know everything I need to know about you," Paul informed her, looking down at the creamy skin and hard-tipped breasts outlined beneath the sheet. "I know that I want you in a way I've never wanted any other woman. I look at you and I ache. I touch you and I feel strong and happy and...whole."

Tricia's heart turned over as she stared at him. His earnest words, the bemused expression on his face, pleased her almost beyond bearing. Could a man really say such things and not mean them?

She pulled herself up short, remembering another handsome face, another man's voice. Once before in her life, she'd fallen victim to a practiced line and later on had nothing but bitter regrets to show for it. If she believed this man's words, would she be any better off? Paul had already made it clear that he wanted her body. He'd also indicated that he wasn't the type to settle down. "I'm glad I make you feel that way, Paul, but desire isn't enough to base a marriage on."

She took a deep breath and revealed the deep inner fear that had yet to be appeased by anything he'd said. "Maybe you weren't really thinking of marriage when you offered to get engaged. Maybe what you want is a way to legitimize our affair while you decide if your sexual attraction to me is going to last for any length of time. Then, if it doesn't, you can leave me behind to make explanations while you go along on your merry way."

Paul knew what lay behind her accusations, but that didn't prevent him from getting angry. "Dammit, woman! I'm not like that slime-ball you got hooked up with in college so don't paint me with the same tarnished brush!''

Tricia recoiled from him in shock, embarrassed color flooding into her cheeks. She knew very well who'd told him the story of her broken engagement. "Grannie had no business discussing my personal life with you.''

"Tricia, you know that she considers anything that affects you her business.''

"I may know it, but I don't have to like it," Tricia retorted.

Paul's lips twitched at her offended expression. "I realize that you won't particularly like hearing this either, but your grandmother hardly keeps a secret of the fact that she wouldn't mind if the two of us got together. She thought it might help the cause if she told me what I might be up against with you because of that other guy.''

"Why would she think you had any interest in this cause of hers?" Tricia wanted to know.

"Because I was so jealous when you walked out that door tonight to meet Larry Wheeler that even a blind man could see it.''

"Oh," Tricia exclaimed, taken aback by his answer. It certainly was a night of revelations, and this was one she'd least expected. It pleased her immensely. When she spoke again, Paul couldn't help but notice the delighted sparkle in her eyes. "So what all did Grannie say to help the cause?''

Keeping back the information he'd gathered about her from another source, Paul recounted his last conversation with Aurie, ending with the observation, "Joe Mangioni was a selfish jerk. He took advantage of you but that doesn't mean I'd do the same. If all I

wanted was your body, I could have had it the first day
I was here. I want more from you, Tricia, much
more.''

Tricia couldn't believe how drastically things had
changed in the course of one day. Paul had worn on
her nerves, her heart and emotions more in the last few
weeks than other man had done in years. She wanted
him desperately and it came as a blessed relief to know
that he felt the same hunger for her.

Even so, there wasn't any future for them and the
sadness that realization brought her was very apparent in her voice. ''You're a loner, Paul. Do you honestly think you'd be happy staying in one place for the
rest of your life? This is my home and I never plan to
leave it again. I've been all over the world and discovered that this farm is where I belong. The man I marry
has to accept that and share in my plans for a home
and a family.''

More than anything, Paul wanted to dispel her ap-
prehensions about him, but he couldn't do so without
being dishonest. After being with her for so short a
time, he couldn't guarantee that they'd live happily
together for the rest of their lives. All he knew was that
he was happy now, happier than he'd ever been in his
life.

''What you say is true, Tricia,'' he conceded, his
mouth going tight as he watched her face fall. ''I've
been on my own since I was sixteen, but in all that time
I never found what it was I was searching for. I want
you to believe me when I tell you that I think I may
have found it tonight. When I made love to you, I felt
like I'd come home. After years of searching, I think
I've finally found where I belong and it isn't a place
but with a person . . . with you.''

"Oh, Paul," Tricia breathed, moved beyond measure, but he didn't wait for her to say more.

"All I'm asking you for is a chance to find out if what we've got is as special as I think it is. Give me that chance, Tricia," he coaxed hoarsely. "Give us both that chance."

Tricia wanted that chance just as much as he did, but didn't know if she had the courage to take it. Her eyes wandered all over him, loving every rippling muscle of his body, every feature of his face. She loved the way he made her feel, his kindness to Grannie, the boyish enthusiasm he displayed each time he was presented with some new aspect of farm life he'd either forgotten or knew nothing about.

Tonight, after long days of wanting and needing, he had made love to her and the beauty, the absolute rightness of it still made her tremble. Her deepest emotions had been locked away for years, yet this man held the key. Knowing that, how could she possibly say no to him? "I want that too, but . . ."

"But you can't risk having an affair." Paul finished for her. "That's why we have to get engaged, Tricia. And the engagement will be a real one. We'll use this time to do what any other engaged couple does. We'll find out if we're really right for each other, if together we can build that future you want."

He reached out his hand to cup her chin and smiled into her eyes. "What do you say?"

She didn't have to say anything. Her answer was right there in her eyes. Paul saw it and responded, "You won't be sorry, Tricia, I promise you. I don't want to do anything to hurt you, or your grandmother or your business."

Tricia believed him, truly believed him and suddenly she was brimming over with excitement. "If we're going to be engaged, then I want to know more about you, Paul Lansing. You've got to admit that I know next to nothing."

"There's not that much to tell." Paul shrugged his shoulders as guilt coiled itself in the pit of his stomach like a snake waiting to strike. What she didn't know couldn't hurt her, but what would happen when she found out the truth?

"Tell me about your family," Tricia suggested hesitantly, prepared to be rebuffed. Ever since that day when they'd brought Smokey home, she'd known that this subject was off-limits, but if he wanted them to have a future, she had to know something of his past.

To her amazement, Paul seemed relieved by that suggestion. Pulling her in front of him, he slid them both back down on the bed. Tricia would've preferred being in a position to watch his expression as he began talking, but her head was resting comfortably on his shoulder and his arms around her waist felt so good that she couldn't bear to move.

"My mother died when I was a baby," he began. "My father got remarried when I was five. My stepmother didn't relate to children very well and to make life easier for my father, I left home when I was sixteen. I joined the service and stayed in for four years. When I was discharged, I bummed around the country on various jobs just like I told you, and that, my dear, is the very mundane and highly uneventful story of my life."

"Uh huh," Tricia mused considerately, then twisted around so abruptly that Paul hadn't a chance of stopping her. In a matter of seconds, he found himself

chest to chest and nose to nose with a woman whose
ferocious expression told him that she wasn't the least
bit satisfied with his tale.

"I've got a slight problem with that pathetic ver-
sion of your life story, mister," she informed him
hotly. "I haven't known you very long but I know
perfectly well that you've never done one mundane or
uneventful thing in your life. Now are you going to
come clean or do I have to apply a little more pressure?"

Since the satiny thigh between his legs was applying
quite enough pressure as it was, Paul was moved to
comply with her heated request. "Okay, okay," he
agreed, starting to laugh as Tricia glared down into his
face.

"I'm really serious about this," she declared, com-
pressing her lips to keep from giggling. With fiendish
relish, she thrust her forearm over his throat as she
brought the full weight of her body down on his chest.
"Having been in this position myself recently, I know
how effective it is so I suggest you start talking."

Paul nodded his head vigorously and Tricia removed her arm from his throat. "Very effective," he
agreed, shifting beneath her so she could feel what her
physical threat had accomplished. "But I'm not sure
it's impressed me with the need to talk."

He gazed down at the lovely pair of breasts against
his chest and groaned, "Maybe you would have had
better luck with this tactic if you weren't so beautifully naked and silky soft to the touch."

"Then I'll just have to try some other means of
persuading you," Tricia said at his lips. "I've got all
night."

"The night's almost over," he reminded her, his breath coming faster and faster as she tantalized his mouth with the tip of her tongue.

"We've got a couple more hours," she teased seductively, rubbing herself against him. "If you talk real fast, we might even have enough time for another enjoyable form of communication."

"Talking can wait," Paul growled. Taking hold of her waist with both hands, he reversed their positions in one swift motion.

Aware that her provocative actions had just backfired in her face, Tricia gasped in protest. "Paul, I didn't intend to..."

"To drive me over the edge? Well, you did, so you'll have to take the consequences," Paul muttered hoarsely, as he bent his head and buried his lips against her throat. Tricia trembled as he used his teeth lightly on her skin.

She tried to prove that he couldn't take control of her so easily by squirming away, but she learned very quickly that he could. He claimed her mouth and her body at the same time. Tricia went completely still beneath the shock of his possession, opened her eyes and found that Paul was gazing down at her, gray eyes flaring with fire.

"You belong to me, Tricia. Whatever happens after tonight, never forget that." Bracing his upper body on his powerful arms, he moved within her, watching her face as he set the rhythm they would take.

"Paul?" Tricia questioned, but then the haze of passion clouded all thought and she couldn't remember which part of his statement had troubled her. She felt taken, possessed, held completely captive by the man staring straight into her eyes as he relentlessly heightened her pleasure.

"Oh," she whispered sharply as the incredible sensations rose higher, so high she thought she might die before reaching culmination. She dug her nails into his shoulders without realizing it. She twisted her hips, arched her back and finally closed her eyes as the tempest hit.

"Open your eyes," Paul demanded, his body taut, his features clenching as he, too, was caught up in the storm. "Watch it happen."

In that one wondrous, excruciating moment before release, Tricia saw his face, his eyes loving her. "I'm yours, Paul," she whispered. "Whatever happens, I'm yours and you're mine."

Though she had never weathered such a tidal wave of emotions in all her life, Paul was the one who took the longest time calming down. Unaware of the effect her poignant words had had on him, Tricia stroked his slick skin, soothing him as the shudders lessened and marveled at the force of his passion.

"I didn't think a man could do that . . . be so loving twice in one night," she told him as he lifted his head away from her breasts.

Paul levered himself off of her. Sprawled on his back, arms beneath his head, he smiled up at the ceiling. For the first time in his recollection, he felt totally content with the world. Without a shadow of a doubt, he knew that the lady in his bed was exactly who he thought she was—a warm, passionate, loving woman.

Tricia wasn't a virgin, but he was almost certain that before tonight, she'd been close to being one. Joseph Mangioni may have taken her innocence, but he was the man who'd provided her first experience with pleasure...and her second—and every one she would ever have from now on.

Of course, when she found out what had brought him to the farm, she was going to be upset, but she'd never be able to walk away from him now. He'd taught her passion, claimed all that feminine fire that burned within her and now she was his. She'd surrendered completely.

"Well, you don't have to look so smug about it," Tricia remarked tartly, knowing she was the subject of his thoughts and certain that she wouldn't like what he was thinking. "I'm sure we haven't broken any records."

"Not yet, but we will," Paul promised in a supremely arrogant tone as his body drifted into a drowsy, complacent state.

Tricia heard a gentle snore. "Paul Lansing! Don't you dare fall asleep on me!"

Paul mumbled something unintelligible.

"I'm warning you. If you don't wake up and talk to me, you're going to regret it!"

"Mmm hmm." Paul smiled briefly in his sleep, then turned over onto his side, completely oblivious to the outraged woman who grabbed up her clothes and stormed out of the room.

At breakfast time, Aurie plunked a generous helping of scrambled eggs on each of their plates but neither Tricia nor Paul noticed. They were too busy staring daggers across the table at each other. On her second trip from the stove, Aurie gave them each more sausages than either one of them ever ate, but they didn't so much as blink. When she served up her freshly baked, homemade cinnamon rolls and they didn't notice the extra trouble she'd gone to on their behalf, she decided it was time to take action. After all, silence never accomplished anything.

"Don't be mad at him, Tricia," Aurie advised gruffly as she took her place between them at the table. "If Paul said something stupid to you when you got in last night it's only because he was jealous because you went out with another man. And Paul, you don't have to worry that Tricia went behind your back and cozied up to Larry. I only made it sound that way because I thought a tiny push might prompt a little action around here."

Satisfied that she had their full attention, she shook her finger under Paul's nose. "For a modern man, you sure are dense when it comes to women. Tricia practically eats you up with her eyes whenever she looks at you. And as for you, my girl—" she turned on her granddaughter "—if you can't see that this poor man is half-crazy about you, then you're as blind as they come."

"Grannie."

"Aurie."

The elderly woman threw up her hands before either of them could continue. "Don't tell me your troubles. What's going on between you two ain't none of my business and I'm not about to get in the middle of it. Now eat up your breakfast and get out to the barn where you can air your differences without a third party listening in. I've already said all I've got to say on the subject!"

Tricia and Paul's eyes locked and as quickly looked away. Paul knew if he caught her glance again he'd burst out laughing and then they'd really be in the

doghouse. Tricia kept her head down, lips twitching
as she picked up her fork and dug into her eggs. She
didn't dare give even the slightest glance at the man
seated across the table from her for fear it would be all
over for them both.

"That's better," Aurie pronounced as she watched
them dig into their food. "Now that we've got that
settled, we can all relax and eat a good breakfast."

Picking up the covered basket from the center of the
table, she announced with a telling sniff, "It's not
every morning I get up at the crack of dawn to bake
homemade rolls, so you two had best enjoy 'em."

"Yes, ma'am," Paul stated meekly as he accepted
the basket and removed what felt like a warm brick
coated with a kind of sticky goo.

When the basket was passed to Tricia, she prayed
for strength and lifted out her grandmother's burnt
offerings. "Nothing like hot cinnamon rolls on a
warm morning. Thanks, Grannie."

"No trouble," Aurie declared, and beamed each of
them a gratified smile. "I'll make another batch tomorrow."

Eight

As he stepped outside, Paul gazed up at the streaky pink clouds on the horizon and took a deep invigorating breath of the crisp morning air. Spring was coming. He didn't need a calendar or an astronomical chart to tell him that they were entering that period between the vernal equinox and the summer solstice. The signs of oncoming change were everywhere.

Riding along with the cold breeze of a mid-March sunrise was the sweet smell of new life. Beneath the paper-thin ice along the graveled driveway, he could see flecks of green growth pushing up from the ground. A week-long warming trend had drastically reduced the size of the snowdrifts and in some spots, the snow had melted completely away.

The trees were still bare, yet their stark branches held buds that only needed a lengthy dose of strong sunlight to burst free. Mornings came earlier, evenings stayed later and in between time, the sky was a bright, cornflower blue.

For the last twenty years of his life, Paul had rarely stopped to notice the passage of seasons, but a farmer was always aware of such things. A man who worked on the land, built an intimate relationship with it and developed an acute sense of the changing cycles. Paul's father, whom he had loved deeply, was such a man. "A time to plant, a time to build, a time to keep, a time to reap, and always time enough to give thanks," Paul quoted out loud, unaware that he'd grasped hold of Tricia's hand as they walked together toward the barn.

"Who said that?" Tricia inquired, smiling at the familiar sentiment.

"My Dad." Paul pulled open the heavy barn door and waited for her to step inside. "Every year in early spring, we'd walk across our fields to determine if it was the right time to start planting. Dad would scoop up a handful of dirt, smell it, and then watch how it fell back to the ground. If it broke into small clods on the way down, he'd say, 'Soil's ready to grow the next generation, Pauly' and then he'd repeat that saying about time."

Paul shrugged his shoulders, a nostalgic look on his face. "I haven't thought about that in years."

"Everyone who's ever lived on a farm has nice memories like that," Tricia said, as she stripped off her coat and hung it up on a wooden peg. "The life of a farmer isn't easy, but being close to nature brings a kind of reward that those who've always lived in the city might never have or even understand. Sometimes, when I watch a farrowing or look over a field of our growing corn, I get this huge lump in my throat. I'm overwhelmed by such a strong sense of peace and belonging that it makes me want to cry for all those unlucky people who live out their entire lives without feeling as if they're a necessary part of anything."

"I've lived a long time feeling that way," Paul admitted, as he removed his jacket and hung it on a peg next to hers. "That's why I was so annoyed with you for running out on me last night. When we made love, I finally felt that kind of peace and belonging. Then, when I woke up and discovered you weren't beside me, the feeling went away."

Tricia nodded. "I was annoyed with you for falling asleep before we could talk. I assumed you'd gotten what you wanted from me and felt no further need to communicate."

Paul reached for two pitchforks and handed one to her. "How could you think that about a man who's so crazy about you even a blind man could see it?"

"Because for a modern man, he's awfully dense when it comes to women," Tricia retorted and they both laughed.

Paul gestured for Tricia to preceed him over the rail of the nearest stall. "We'd better get to work. Neither one of us is going to last very long on the amount of sleep we got last night."

"That's for sure," Tricia agreed with a wide yawn.

Once inside the stall, they worked companionably for several minutes, then Paul tiptoed across the stall for a peek at the participants in his first farrowing. Old number eleven was asleep in the next stall along with her newborn litter of eight. They all appeared healthy and Paul felt a strong measure of pride with his accomplishment.

Even so, when the sow cocked open one eye, he immediately jumped back out of her sight.

"You'll have to stand up to Betty Sue sometime," Tricia warned, stifling a giggle. "Otherwise she'll walk all over you every chance she gets."

"Considering the number of times that six hundred pound mama has stepped on me already, I think I'll wait a while before confronting her with my masculine superiority."

Tricia laughed. "You know what Grannie says, dogs look up to you, cats look down on you, but pigs think you're their equal."

Paul contemplated that sage advice for a second, recalled how it had felt to be smashed up against the side of a stall by a grunting old sow and quipped, "Having the respect of one out of three ain't that bad."

"Coward," Tricia teased as Paul moved away from Betty Sue's stall and started pitching straw in the opposite corner.

"In some ways, I guess I am," Paul admitted, leaning on the handle of his pitchfork. "I know I'm having a heck of a time working up my courage to tell you all you want to know about me."

Tricia sent him such a sweet, understanding smile that Paul decided to brave it out. "My stepmother, Doreen, never acted like a mother, though she made me call her that. I thought the only reason she insisted was that she knew how much I hated it."

"And she also hated dogs," Tricia guessed.

Paul shrugged. "She hated Smokey because I loved him. I know now that a lot of her behavior came out of her desperation to take over my real mother's place in Dad's life. My father made Doreen feel that she

could never do that with him or with me. I don't think
Dad realized what he was doing, but he was always
making comparisons between Doreen and my mother
and Doreen always came up short.''

"So she took her frustration with her husband out
on you?''

"I'm sure I seemed like the perfect scapegoat," Paul
said with far less emotion than the statement implied.
Sensing Tricia's questioning eyes on him, he elabor-
ated, "I was the spitting image of my mother. I have
her eyes, her nose, the exact same color hair. Whenever I smiled, my Dad reminded Doreen that I'd in-
herited my dimples from his beautiful first wife. After
a time, I didn't smile very often because Doreen took
great pleasure in wiping it off my face.''

"She hit you!" Tricia was appalled. She could feel
a great deal of compassion for the second wife who
always had to live up to the shining image of another
woman, but that empathy didn't expand to include
child abuse.

Paul pitched a heavy forkful of soiled straw over the
rail onto the electric conveyer. "Sometimes," he confirmed, without looking at her. "She couldn't stand
the sight of me, and in a way I can't blame her. At the
time, I didn't understand why she hated me so much.
I remember once when I was seven, Doreen took me
to the barber and had all my hair shaved off. She told
my Dad that she'd instructed the man to cut it short
since we were having such hot weather and he'd mis-
understood her. I knew better. When the school bus
came to pick me up the next day, all the kids laughed
and Doreen joined right in.''

Tricia put down her fork. "Where was your father during this? Where was he when she hit you and made fun of you?"

"Out working in the barn or the fields. I don't really remember," was all Paul said, but Tricia heard the resentment that lay behind those words. She tried to picture him as a small boy living under the conditions he described and was overcome by pity. "Doreen threatened to do even worse things to you if you complained to your father, didn't she?"

Paul's response was a curt "Yeah" and with it came the message that he was all through talking.

Tricia's heart went out to him. Without a second's hesitation, she dropped her pitchfork and walked across the space that separated them. Needing to comfort him, she threw her arms around his waist. Paul went rigid at her touch, but she refused to let go of him until she'd had her say. "Don't you dare call yourself a coward for keeping quiet all those years. None of what happened to you was your fault. You were only a child and whatever you had to do to protect yourself was the right thing to do. Leaving home when you did was the right thing, the absolutely best thing for all concerned and I'm proud of you for making such a courageous decision. I never would've had the strength to strike out on my own like you did."

Astonished by her perception, Paul was too choked up with emotion to say anything. He'd deliberately downplayed his feelings, yet Tricia had picked up on every one of them. She'd even known of the painful struggle he'd had maintaining his sense of self while his stepmother had continually emasculated him with her cruel threats. Even after he'd left home, he'd suffered with the knowledge that he'd knuckled under to her out of fear, almost a fully grown man, yet too scared to do anything but run away.

Maybe that was why he'd taken such a high-risk job. He'd had to prove to himself and to others that he wasn't a coward, that he could stand up to any challenge no matter how dangerous. Indeed, as time went on, the bigger the challenge and the greater the danger, the better he liked it.

Tricia's arms tightened around him as if sensing that he'd drifted away from her in his thoughts. Immediately, Paul let go of his pitchfork and hugged her back, resting his chin on the top of her head. In a short span of time, Tricia had become more dear to him than any job ever could be. She was the biggest and best challenge he'd ever faced and failing to meet it would be his greatest failure. He couldn't allow that to happen.

"I think you should know that I love you, Paul," Tricia declared, pressing her cheek against his shirt. She heard his response in the thundering beat of his heart and she was glad that she'd spoken the words that, for the remainder of last night, had been tossing and turning around in her head while she'd tossed and turned on the mattress.

Paul held her close, wishing he could give her the same gift that she'd just given him, but unable to do so with a clear conscience. Until she knew what had brought him into her life and forgiven him for deceiving her, he had to avoid a vow that should only be uttered when there was total honesty between two people. When that time came, he would tell her of his love. He prayed it would be soon. "I think you should know that hearing you love me makes me very, very happy."

He felt her lips curve upward in a smile and he
blessed the fates that had sent him to her. Because of
the unconditional love and security Tricia had enjoyed all her life, she felt free to convey it to others—
to him. She offered her love unselfishly without demanding an equal return.

But you'll have all my love, Paul promised her silently. *As soon as possible, I'll make certain that you'll
have that and much more.*

It would take a lifetime to repay her for all she'd
done for him. Because out of her compassion, he'd
found out that he'd been carrying an unnecessary
burden around with him for most of his adult life.
Tricia had made him see what no one else had, including himself.

It had been strength and not weakness that had
caused him to leave home at the age of sixteen. He had
been strong and his father weak, so weak that he'd
turned a blind eye on his wife's cruelty and his son's
suffering.

Knowing now what a real family should be like, it
was still hard for Paul to admit the truth, but he realized that he needed to dilute the poison that had been
eating away at him for so many years. Truth was, he'd
hated his father almost as much as he'd loved him. In
all of the eleven years Paul had endured Doreen's
harsh treatment, Ralph Lansing had never once inter-
fered. Paul had Tricia to thank for helping him to accept his mixed feelings toward his father without being
ripped apart.

In the short time he'd spent with her and her
grandmother, he'd learned so much about giving and
forgiving. Because of them, he could rid himself of his
self-defeating attitude toward life and redirect all his

misdirected priorities. On the Courteau farm, he'd finally found the answers he was seeking.

"Have you ever been back to see your family?" Tricia ventured, hating to ask, but hoping to reach the point where they could put all his painful memories behind them so they could continue moving forward.

"Both my dad and my stepmother were killed in a car accident a few months ago," Paul said, trusting Tricia enough to let his troubled feelings show. "In over twenty years, I never went back to see them. Even so, they left me the farm. An angry part of me still didn't want anything to do with the place that held so many bad memories for me, so I sold it. But there was another part of me that loved that farm and will always regret that decision. In some strange kind of way, I was tied to that land and the people who'd been on it. I felt I owed it to my dad and the generations of other Lansings who had lived out their lives there to keep the farm going. Don't you feel like that about this place?"

"Yes." Tricia lifted her head from his shirt, her big brown eyes brimming with moisture. "But those people will always be with you, Paul, wherever you go. As a wise man once said, a generation of men is like a generation of leaves scattered to the wind. Some fail, some flourish and bring forth new life, some simply perish, but they all move on in one way or another."

Paul lifted his hand and brushed his fingers down the side of her face. "Like leaves scattered to the wind," he repeated her phrasing to himself as if testing its taste in his mouth, then he smiled. "The wind brought this man here to you."

"And I'm so glad it did," Tricia murmured, just before Paul lowered his head and kissed her.

At first, his lips were warm and exquisitely tender. Tricia closed her eyes with a soft sigh and reveled in the glorious feel of them. But then, Paul drew her more firmly against him and in that instant, the kiss changed from being sweet to wildly intoxicating.

Paul's tongue caressed her, probed into the honeyed darkness of her mouth. His chest pressed against her soft breasts and Tricia could feel the hardness of muscle and the warmth of his flesh. In helpless hunger, she crushed her mouth against his. Paul's mouth opened under her insistence and his body relayed a blatant message to her with an achingly slow hungry rhythm.

The gentle hands at her waist began to explore her in a new way as his fingers slid inside her blouse. Tricia clung to him, crying out when he flattened his hand against her breast and took the hard nipple into his palm. Her heart seemed to stop beating.

"Tricia, you know what's going to happen if we go on like this," Paul whispered ruefully as he lifted his mouth away from hers. "I'm going to haul you down on the nearest haystack and all the little critters in the barn are going to have to wait a long, long time for their breakfast."

Tricia considered ignoring the responsibility, giving in to the flaming desire that raged within her, and desire won. She looked up into the smoldering gray eyes gazing down at her and murmured raggedly, "The way I'm feeling right now, they wouldn't have to wait very long."

Paul appeared to be slightly stunned by her candor. His brows shot up and he stared down at her as if he'd heard wrong. "Are you saying what I think you're saying? You want to make love right here and now?"

"Don't you?" Tricia inquired, a tiny furrow developing on her forehead. Maybe Paul didn't appreciate aggressive women. Maybe he was just like Joe, who'd made it patently clear that in sexual matters, a woman's requirements were always subordinate to a man's, that she should take a submissive role. Maybe all men felt like that and there was something wrong with her for being so immodest about her own needs.

She remembered Paul's reaction that first day when they'd ridden to town in his truck and she'd thrown herself at him. Did he consider her present conduct equally licentious? She was sure that was it when he took a step back.

"Tricia," he began the explanation she didn't want to hear.

"Forget it. I'm sorry if I've offended you," she interrupted him in a very small voice, her cheeks burning with embarrassment.

If anything, Paul looked even more stunned. "That's the second time you've made that kind of nonsensical remark to me," he burst out gruffly, his hands grasping hold of her shoulders. "I don't know who gave you the idea that expressing your desires is a turnoff to a man, but whoever did ought to be shot. I let you get away with thinking that the last time because you were so upset and I thought I'd only make matters worse by saying anything, but I won't let that happen again."

Tricia's mouth dropped open as Paul grasped her hand and strode toward the rail. He kept hold of her as they climbed out of the stall. As soon as they were both standing on the other side, he scooped her up and walked purposefully down the center aisle. When they reached the pile of fresh hay stacked in a nearby corner, he lowered her on it and brought himself down beside her, propping his head up on an elbow so she could see his face.

"Lady, you can seduce me anytime, anyplace, anywhere and I promise you, I'll love every minute of it. The only reason I hesitated taking you up on your offer was that I couldn't quite believe I could be so lucky. Here you are, about as innocent as they come, yet you're totally honest about your feelings. When you want me, you're not afraid to show me how much and that's the best gift a woman could ever give to her man."

Tricia smiled tremulously. "It is?"

"Yes, it is." Paul's tone was final.

"Then let me show you some more." With a joyful laugh, Tricia rolled over on top of him.

Perfectly willing to participate, Paul drew her mouth down to his. Tricia made sure he couldn't question her enjoyment of his kiss or be left in any doubt about what she wished to happen next. By the time they came up for air, she'd already unbuttoned his shirt and unzipped his jeans. "Are you sure you wouldn't rather be with a woman who had more experience?" she inquired teasingly, feeling his shudder as her fingers journeyed down his bare chest.

Paul stifled a groan at the warm circular motions of her palm on his stomach. "I'm sure," he managed, but only by gritting his teeth.

Her brown eyes adored him as she continued her exploration, completely enthralled in her task. Taking a kneeling position beside him, she drew his shirt off his shoulders and cast it aside. Paul encouraged her with his eyes, lifting his hips to assist her in removing the rest of his clothes. And then she was able to see the magnificence she'd only gotten a glimpse of the night before.

His body was beautifully made. He'd been some-place warm recently for his skin was still lightly tanned. His muscles were hard, yet supple and they rippled beneath her touch. The bronze disks of his nipples, nestled in swirls of dark hair, intrigued her. She had never been aware of such maleness. Sheer maleness. Mature, powerfully packaged maleness.

"How do you know I'm such a beginner?" Tricia asked softly, fascinated by the whirl of dark hair that arrowed downward from his navel. Slowly, she trailed her fingers along that textured path, breathlessly aware that her movements increased the already impressive proof of his arousal. "Was my inexperience so ob-vious?"

"It was obvious that everything you felt last night was brand-new," Paul said, but then her fingers found him and all he could do was gasp in pleasure. Before losing what little control he had left, he lifted his arms, his fingers shaking as they fumbled for the buttons on her blouse.

In a strangled tone he told her, "And today it's just as obvious that you're a very fast learner."

Tricia was allowed one small expression of femi-nine delight before she succumbed to a vast new array of wondrously gratifying lessons.

"Now if you two don't look like something the cat dragged in," Aurie chided as Paul and Tricia took their places at the kitchen table.

Very much aware of Aurie's disapproving eyes on him, Paul leaned across the table and picked a stem of hay out of Tricia's black hair. "You don't have to get

out the shotgun, Aurie," he declared with a wide grin.
"We're engaged."

Immediately all smiles, Aurie clapped her hands
together and exclaimed, "Well, by the looks of it, that
decision didn't come any too soon. But I'm so glad it
did, so terribly glad for both of you."

Still trying to deal with her astonishment over Paul's
announcement, Tricia completely ignored her grandmother's joyful reaction to the news. Last night they'd
agreed to become engaged, but nothing further had
been said on the subject today and she'd assumed
they'd postpone making any public declarations about
their relationship until they were more certain about
it themselves.

On the other hand, she was the one who had expressed her reluctance to have an affair, and since their
relationship was perfectly obvious to Grannie, what
else had she expected Paul to say when the older
woman hit him with the evidence of their newfound
intimacy?

Paul was perplexed by Tricia's worried expression.
"We're pretty happy about it, too, aren't we, Tricia?"

Tricia heard the uncertainty behind his question and
found herself agreeing even if she still had a few reservations concerning their future together. "Very
happy."

Aurie plunked herself down at the table. "Now
mind you, I'm pretty modern in my thinking so it
don't bother me none that you two have placed the
cart a bit ahead of the horse, but Mack and Leona
haven't moved with the times. They should be here
real soon, so maybe you two had better put off eating
dinner for awhile and go spiffy yourselves up some."

"Mom and Dad are coming here!" Tricia cried in sudden panic. "Now? Today?"

"Yessiree, they called me up around eight and said they'd be on the road by eleven," Aurie said. "I 'spect they thought it was high time they met Paul, since we've been raving about him ever since he got here. Can't blame 'em for being curious."

"Who's been raving?" Tricia glared accusingly at her grandmother. "Not me. I haven't made more than a passing mention of Paul when I've spoken to them."

Aurie was taken aback by Tricia's reproachful tone. "Seeing as how you just got yourself engaged to the man, that strikes me as sort of strange. Don't you think your folks want to hear all about the person you're going to marry? If it were me, I'd be dying to give them all the romantic details."

Tricia groaned in defeat and slumped back in her chair. She shot a miserable glance at the wall clock, confirming that she was almost out of time. In less than a half hour, her parents were going to walk through that door and start an inquisition. Worse than that, the majority of their probing questions were going to be directed at Paul. "Oh, Grannie. How could you do this to us?"

"Do what?" Paul's terse query cut through the heavy atmosphere like a sharp knife.

Startled by his anger, Tricia met his cold gray gaze and realized that he'd totally misread her reaction to the news of her parent's imminent arrival. "Paul, you don't understand—"

"What's to understand?" Paul demanded harshly. "You've made it clear that you don't want your parents to know anything about me. Apparently, all I am to you is a *passing* fancy who doesn't warrant any more than a *passing* mention."

"That's not true," Tricia insisted beseechingly. "That's not how I feel at all. It's just that—"

Paul was too furious to listen to her excuses. Shoving back his chair, he stood up from the table and raged, "It's just that you aren't ready to take out any advertisements about us. So far, all I've done is given you a good toss in the hay but you don't think that's enough of a commitment on my part, right? Well, you weren't saying that this morning, lady! This morning, what I had to offer was plenty good enough for you."

"Oh...my," Aurie breathed plaintively, pressing a hand over her heart. "Guess I'm not as modern-minded as I thought. I don't think I'm up to hearing this so I'm going in the other room until you've got it all settled." The elderly woman moved to comply with that decision faster than Tricia had ever seen her move in her life.

As shocked by Paul's words as her grandmother, Tricia covered her face in her hands. "Did you have to be so crude? Don't you have a single shred of common decency?"

The self-condemnation Paul felt at offending Aurie's sensibilities only increased his anger with Tricia. "Me? What about you? Or weren't you the woman who less than an hour ago claimed she loved me while she was ripping off my clothes?"

Tricia's hands fell away from her face as her humiliated feelings were instantly replaced by ire. "I do love you, you bad-mannered jerk and if you'd calm down long enough to listen, I could explain the excellent reason I have for not wanting my parents to think we're engaged. Though why, I should bother explaining is beyond me! After this little episode, you deserve everything you're going to get when they arrive."

"What's that supposed to mean?" Paul inquired in a somewhat less ferocious tone of voice. "What am I going to get?"

Under the present circumstances, Tricia took great satisfaction in telling him. "Questions, Mr. Lansing. My parents are going to ask you a million and one, indepth, highly personal questions in order to ascertain whether or not you qualify as good marriage prospect for their beloved only daughter. And believe me, if you mention that you're honorable intentions rose out of a good toss in the hay, you won't live to toss again."

Staggered by her speech, Paul quit pacing in front of the table and sank down in the closest chair. "And that's why you were so upset when I said we were engaged?"

"Yes."

"You weren't trying to deny..."

"No!"

"Oh." Paul winced at her emphatic tone. "Tricia, I'm really sorry. I never should have said what I did in front of your grandmother."

"No, you shouldn't have," Tricia agreed. "And if you think you're sorry now, just wait and see how you're going to feel once my parents get done with you."

"He'll live!" Aurie shouted from the living room. "That is if you both get a move on pretty darned quick. I think I see a car coming up the road."

Tricia ran for the back stairs, not even stopping to see if Paul was behind her. "Don't say I didn't warn you," she called back to him over her shoulder as she gained the second floor and dashed down the hall to her room.

Nine

___

"If I were twenty years younger, I'd think about coming back to the farm and starting over," Mack Courteau told Paul as they walked side by side down the muddy drive. "But it's too late for me now. Another five years at the plant and I can retire. Leona's got her heart set on doing some traveling, something we were never able to do when we were farming.

"Maybe we'll even take to living down south in a warmer climate during the winter. We spent a few nice days in Florida this year. I sure wouldn't mind trying my hand at some deep-sea fishing, and Leona thinks living by the ocean would be paradise."

Since the man didn't appear to require a response to anything he'd said thus far, Paul didn't make one. They continued walking along amiably and Mack continued talking about inconsequential matters. As they reached the line of fence between the farrowing barn and the hog shed, Mack inquired, "You sure you want to be a farmer? It's not an easy life."

"I'm sure," Paul said.

Mack seemed satisfied with that brief response for he thrust his hands into the pockets of his overcoat and began telling Paul about a new type of high-growth hog feed he'd read about in *Scientific American* magazine. The longer the man talked, the closer Paul came to deciding that Tricia had been apprehensive for nothing.

The minute her father had invited him to come outside for a walk, Paul had expected an interrogation, but that hadn't happened and it was beginning to look as if it wasn't going to. Tricia had warned him of an inquisition, but thus far, neither Mack nor Leona Courteau had asked him one single question that might be considered as none of their business.

When Aurie had informed them about Tricia's engagement, the couple had seemed genuinely happy for their daughter and with nary another word had offered their hearty congratulations. Over coffee and cake, they had exchanged the normal pleasantries between people who were meeting each other for the first time. Yet, each time Paul had caught Tricia's eye, she'd cast him a look of impending doom.

Ignoring her unease, Paul had involved himself in the friendly conversation, taking an immediate liking to both of Tricia's parents. He'd noticed right off that Tricia took after her father's side of the family in temperament and her mother's side in looks.

At fifty-five, Leona Courteau was a soft-spoken, retiring woman, still attractively slender, and with only a small amount of gray in her short black hair. Her beautiful eyes were just as large and the exact shade of brown as Tricia's. Mack Courteau had the thin, wiry build of a French-Canadian trapper, a quick wit, infectious laugh and his mother's snappy hazel eyes.

From the first moment after meeting them, it was perfectly obvious to Paul that they loved their daughter very much. It was equally apparent that Tricia shared the same feeling for them. Then why, Paul wanted to know, had she feared their reaction to the news of their engagement and warned him to expect the worst?

"Course, any kind of new, experimental feed's bound to be expensive," Mack was saying. "Still, it might be worth your looking into."

"I'll do that," Paul replied agreeably.

"Once you two are married, son, will you want Tricia to keep on with this consignment business of hers?" Mack asked.

Paul gave a slight start at the man's matter-of-fact tone. There was no longer any doubt that he'd been accepted as a future son-in-law. Paul could only wish he felt as secure in the role as Mack assumed him to be.

"Tricia really enjoys what she's doing," he said. "I don't see any reason why she shouldn't continue it after we're married. If that's what she wants to do, she's got my full support."

Mack clapped Paul affectionately on the shoulder. "I'm happy you feel that way. You can't run a good marriage when two people are pulling in opposite directions. Tricia's got a good head for business and in another couple of years, my bet is she'll turn in a tidy profit. With the economy down like it is, you'll need that extra income to keep this farm operating in the black."

Since Tricia had told him that her father hadn't demonstrated much faith in her ability to make her business a success, Paul was surprised by this show of support. His feelings must have been apparent on his face for Mack chuckled. "I can see my daughter's been complaining about my negative attitude toward her business."

"She gave me the impression that you had reservations about her chances for making a go of things," Paul admitted.

Mack grinned. "The best way to convince my daughter to do something up right is to tell her you don't think she can. Course, that's not to say I wasn't worried about her biting off more than she could chew. I'll admit your announcement today took a big load off my mind. Besides being as stubborn as her grandmother, my daughter is as loyal as they come. To keep this farm from being sold out from under my mother's feet, she'd sell her soul to the devil."

Just in case the man was wondering if he had any connections with the netherworld, Paul stated firmly, "I realize that I haven't got the personal attachment to this place that Tricia does, but I'd never allow that to happen. In a very short span of time, the future of this farm has become almost as important to me as it is to her."

"Glad to hear it," Mack said. A few yards farther on, he remarked conversationally, "You know, there's not many young men who'd take to the idea of having an old lady living with him and his new wife, especially one who's as outspoken and set in her ways as my mother."

Paul laughed. "As long as I clean my plate and remember to wear my boots, Aurie and I will get along just fine."

Mack grinned. "You got that right."

A few moments later, Mack opened a gate in the fence and Paul had to quicken his pace to keep up with the older man as he began striding across the stockyard. "When I left, Ma sold off some animals, but you and Amos might want to think about enlarging this area and increasing the size of the herd."

Paul missed the inquisitive glance Mack cast his way as he responded to the mention of Amos's name. "According to Tricia, Amos is the best hog man in the country and I'd be wise to take whatever advice he's got to offer."

"Amos is a good man," Mack allowed, then moved on to another topic.

Paul was just beginning to suspect that he was being guided down the primrose path by an expert hand when Mack brought up the subject of money and his suspicion was confirmed. "I expect one of these days, you and Tricia will want to buy out my share of this place."

"Actually, we haven't thought that far ahead," Paul acknowledged warily.

"Well, if you ever feel ready to buy, let me know," Mack offered. "I'm sure we'll be able to work out something. To my way of thinking, a man should own the land he works on."

"I agree and I've accumulated enough cash to offer you a fair price if and when that time comes, but as yet, we haven't even set a date for the wedding," Paul reminded him.

"Now that the weather's warming up a bit, the hogs can get outside more," Mack said, switching subjects again as they reached the hogshed. Standing off to one side, he released the holding gate and both men watched as a sea of pigs moved out into the yard. "Ma said you weren't that familiar with hogs."

"I'm learning more all the time." Paul crossed his arms over his chest and leaned back against the wall of the shed. "On my first day here I was informed of all the advantages there are in raising hogs over other animals. So far, I'm inclined to agree with that conclusion."

Tongue in cheek, Mack said, "Ma's extremely well versed on that subject."

"I'll say," Paul verified, good-naturedly.

"Well, we'd better get back to the ladies," Mack announced with undisguised finality and promptly started heading back to the house.

Paul stared after him, no longer quite so certain that he'd been right in assuming that the last few minutes of conversation had been some sort of a test. He was even more unsettled by the thought that if it had been, he had no idea whether or not he'd passed it.

"You coming?" Mack called back to him, his poker-faced expression giving Paul no clue as to his thoughts.

Confused, Paul shrugged his shoulders. "I'm right behind you."

As soon as they rejoined the women, Paul's confusion was immediately cleared up. Upon entering the living room, Mack went straight over to his wife who was seated on the couch and declared, "You don't have to worry, Mother. Paul's got plenty of money of his own and he genuinely wants to make a go of this place."

"What did I tell you, Leona?" Aurie remarked smugly, looking up from her knitting as Mack sat down next to his wife on the couch. "Paul's a good man."

"We had to learn that for ourselves, Mother Courteau," Leona said, brown eyes encouraging her husband to continue with his assessments.

Listening from the doorway, Paul couldn't decide if he should find a chair for himself or leave the room. Being discussed as if he weren't present was a new experience for him and damned disconcerting. He didn't know if he wanted to hear the rest of this embarrassing conversation or not.

"Oh, no, you don't," Tricia hissed under her breath, coming up beside Paul and grabbing hold of his hand to prevent his escape back into the kitchen. "I gave you fair warning and now we're in this thing together."

Against his better judgment, Paul allowed himself to be pulled away from the doorway. Reluctantly, he sat down in one of the chairs facing the couch, just in time to hear Leona say she was glad to hear he wasn't some fast-talking, vagrant gigolo.

Perched on the arm of his chair, Tricia sighed dramatically and whispered, "I'm so relieved."

Paul glared balefully up at her, trying to remove his hand from her tight grip, but she refused to let it go. "I can't wait to hear the rest of this," she breathed softly, her expression gleeful.

Oblivious to the byplay going on between Tricia and Paul, Mack observed, "And we don't have to be concerned about mother's welfare. Nothing's going to

change for either her or Amos. Paul's all in favor of
them going on living here. As for Tricia, Paul says she
can keep on working just as long as she wants to.''

"How gracious of you," Tricia muttered to Paul
behind her closed hand.

Paul rolled his eyes at her, and shook his head as
Mack continued, "Beyond that, the man's wise
enough to know when he's hearing some good advice
and seems smart enough to take it.''

Tricia leaned over and whispered in Paul's ear.
"Spilled your guts to him, didn't you?''

"And I never even felt the knife," Paul whispered
back resignedly. "Your dad's a very smooth operator.''

Tricia gave him an I-told-you-so look, then released his hand and hopped off the chair. "So, Mom,
Dad, now that you're sure I haven't hooked myself up
with a real loser, what do you say to opening up a
bottle of the grape and doing a little celebrating?''

Leona tutted, "Darling, we never once worried that
you'd gotten hooked up with a loser.''

Mack confessed dryly, "No, it was more like two or
three times.''

Paul groaned.

Tricia giggled.

Aurie stood up from her rocking chair and proclaimed happily, "I bought a bottle of wine at the
grocery store just for this occasion. I'll go get us some
glasses.''

The next two weeks flew by as everyone in the family helped Tricia get ready to show her special mer-
chandise at the country craft fair in Chicago.
Throughout the entire period, Paul and Tricia had lit-

tle opportunity to be alone. By the time Paul finished evening chores and Tricia finished dealing with the steady stream of potential consignees who'd heard about her upcoming trip and wanted their wares to be included in the fair, they were both too tired to require anything more than a warm meal and a soft bed.

Twenty-four hours before the two-day event was scheduled to begin, they set off for Chicago in Paul's truck. Ten hours later, Paul smiled at the anticipatory expression on Tricia's face as he drove the pickup off the Dan Ryan Expressway and onto Michigan Avenue. The closer they'd gotten to downtown Chicago, the more restless she'd become.

"It's another ten blocks or so to the convention center," he teased. "Think you can hold onto your patience that long?"

"Huh?" Tricia pulled her gaze back inside the truck.

Paul laughed. "The way you're tramping down on that imaginary gas pedal under your foot, I get the feeling that I'm not driving fast enough for you. Would you prefer to take over the wheel?"

Tricia glanced down at her right foot, which was definitely pressed against the floor. Wrinkling her nose, she looked over at Paul. "So I'm a little over-anxious. Wouldn't you be if you were in my shoes?"

"I promise, we've got plenty of time to set up your booth before the fair opens tomorrow. We can work all night if we have to," he assured her.

Tricia nodded, but then sat up very straight. "I forgot to load Millie Talbot's enameled roses! The box was in the dining room instead of on the porch and I forgot all about it."

"That's just where I found them," Paul informed her blithely. "And I packed them in with those funny-looking blue things you're so convinced will sell like hotcakes."

Tricia sighed in relief. "Bless you, and whatever you think, Betty Young's lacquered milkweed center-pieces are destined to be a very hot item."

"If you say so," Paul replied equitably.

A few minutes later, Paul spotted a sign for the convention center and turned right. Three blocks farther on he drove the truck into the center's huge, crowded parking lot.

Aware that they'd finally reached their destination after what had seemed like an endless drive, Tricia sat poised on the edge of her seat. Her hand curled around the door handle, she was prepared to make a quick exit.

Paul advised purposefully, "You will kindly stay put inside this truck until I locate the unloading zone."

"Yes, sir." Tricia leaned back on the seat, but her eyes remained glued on the block-long, one-story brick building outside the windshield. "There it is over there. See those diagonal yellow lines right in front of those double doors?"

"I see them."

"Great!" Tricia enthused. "If you turn the truck around and back up, we can start unloading right away."

"And there shall be no rest for the weary," Paul grumbled, as he followed her instructions. "After ten hours on the road, wouldn't you at least like a cup of coffee or maybe a sandwich before we go to work?"

Tricia was too excited to be hungry, but that was no excuse for depriving Paul. "I'm sorry. The last time we stopped was for lunch and..." She glanced at her watch, stricken by the amount of time that had passed since they'd eaten their last meal. "And that was over seven hours ago! You poor thing, you must be starving and you never said a word."

Paul rolled down the window, stuck out his head and maneuvered the rear end of the truck as close to the unloading docks as he could. When he was satisfied, he pulled his head back inside, and turned off the engine. Looking over at her, he boasted in a self-mocking tone, "Noble men like myself are renowned for making such unselfish gestures."

"You are noble," Tricia readily agreed. "And patient and kind and generous and..."

Paul immediately regretted his flippant choice of words, and had to suffer in silence as Tricia regaled him with a list of flowery compliments. He doubted she'd think he was so noble when she found out why he'd tried so hard to make himself indispensable to her. He certainly didn't feel noble, generous or kind. He felt like a low-down, conniving wolf masquerading as a gentle, harmless sheep.

Eyeing his uncomfortable expression, Tricia reaffirmed, "Really, Paul, I mean it. I don't know what I would have done without you this past week. Without all your help, I'd be more of a nervous wreck than I already am and I want you to know how grateful I am to you."

"You would have done just fine without me," Paul said, unable to look at her. "If you want to thank somebody, thank your dad for taking off work and doing the chores while we're gone. It was your mom who drove all over creation picking up all your inventory and Aurie who labeled all the items for sale. All I

did was offer you the use of my truck and to drive you
to Chicago.''

Tricia shook her head. ''Of course, I'm grateful to
them, too, but you're being far too modest. While I
was getting everything organized for this trip, you did
all the chores. You built all those crates I needed and
loaded them for me and now you're going to help me
set up and work my booth. But beyond the physical,
you've given me all the understanding and emotional
support I could possibly ask from anyone.''

Enough was enough, Paul concluded in growing
self-derision, ashamed of the glowing picture she was
painting of him. To prevent her from continuing, he
said, ''In the next two days, you'll probably wish to
withdraw that flattering statement for I have no intention of getting beyond the physical. My reasons for
coming with you were entirely selfish and motivated
by sheer lust. It's been too long since we've made love
and I want your gorgeous body, lady. I knew if I came
with you, we'd have a nice big hotel room all to ourselves where I can have you without the constant threat
of interruption.''

Tricia giggled, finding nothing wrong with his
seemingly dishonorable motivation. ''What a lovely
sentiment and I heartily agree with every word you
said. Why else do you think I let you come? I've been
beside myself with frustration and I want to have your
gorgeous body, too, at the earliest opportunity.''

Unfortunately, they were kept so busy over the next
two days that there was no time for even the briefest
romantic interlude. They'd spent the remainder of the
first night and several hours into the next morning
unloading the truck and setting up the booth to Tricia's specifications. After a short sleep in their hotel

room and a hastily eaten breakfast, they'd returned to the fair at 7:00 a.m. and stayed until the midnight closing.

The second day was much like the first. They were amazed by the enormous crowd that swarmed around Tricia's booth like hungry locusts, carrying off every item in sight. Sales were so brisk and things so hectic that Tricia hadn't even noticed that Paul had waited on the same customer, a short, bald, middle-aged man, a number of times each day.

With nothing left to sell, Tricia couldn't have been happier when the fair was declared officially over Tuesday night at 6:00 p.m. It took another hour for her and Paul to clean out their booth and pack the truck, but then they were free to go back to their hotel where they enjoyed a leisurely dinner before retiring to their room.

"After this, I would say that Courteau Country Crafts is destined to be a smashing success, wouldn't you?" Tricia inquired dreamily, smiling up at the ceiling as she waited for Paul to finish his shower and join her in the king-size bed. When she didn't get an answer to her question, she propped herself up on her forearms. Paul was just stepping out of the bathroom, but he was still wearing all his clothes. "For a man who's so hot for my body, you sure are taking your sweet time coming to bed."

"Have you seen the keys to the truck?" Paul asked, forcing his eyes away from the provocative, womanly curves exposed by her black silk teddy and the equally provocative smile that went with them, as he began searching the pockets of his charcoal gray slacks. "If you don't have them, I must have left them in the ignition."

"I don't have them," Tricia said, not anywhere near as concerned about the problem as Paul appeared to be. To her astonishment, his handsome features were tight with worry. "There's no reason to look so concerned. The truck is parked safely in the hotel garage. It'll still be there in the morning even if you did leave the keys in the ignition."

"Don't I wish," Paul grumbled, as he picked up his sports jacket and rifled the pockets. "The keys aren't in here, either. I'd better go down to the parking garage and have a look."

"Now?"

"Of course now," Paul said, shooting her a look of exasperation. "Do you want to take the chance of waking up and finding the truck stolen?"

"Who would possibly want to steal an old, beaten-up pickup truck?"

"I don't know, but someone might," Paul retorted defensively, and Tricia suddenly realized that something was bothering him besides a missing set of keys. He was pacing around like a caged tiger.

"So I'm going," he stated, the brusque edge in his tone telling her that he would have liked to say more but for some reason didn't dare.

"So it seems," Tricia replied, trying to decipher the strange expression on his face, the sudden intensity in his gaze. His hand was grasped around the door handle, but he seemed oddly hesitant to leave. "Paul, is something wrong?"

Instantly, a shutter came down over his face and he shook his head. "Nothing's wrong. I'll be back as soon as I find the keys, okay?"

Tricia frowned at the way he'd phrased the question. "Meaning if they're not in the truck, you're going to keep on searching?"

"If they're not there, I'll take a look around the garage and the lobby. I might even have dropped them in the restaurant when we had dinner."

"So, what you're telling me is that you might be gone awhile."

Tricia could tell that he disliked telling her that just about as much as she disliked hearing it, but he did so anyway. "It shouldn't take much longer than an hour."

"An hour!" Tricia couldn't hide her disbelief, nor her hurt.

Jaw like granite, Paul admitted through clenched teeth, "No more than two. I promise."

"No more than two," Tricia repeated dumbly.

"Tricia, I..." Paul took a step toward the bed, then stopped himself. "I'll be back as soon as I can," he said tersely. "And don't worry, sweetheart, we'll talk."

"We'll talk," Tricia mumbled, glancing down at her low-cut bodice, then back up at the empty room. She was going to have a few words to say to the saleswoman who'd sold her this skimpy item of intimate apparel. Without giving more than a passing glance to the sexy teddy that was supposedly guaranteed to entice a man, Paul had simply walked out on her!

He'd also promised to come back, but obviously his plans for later weren't anywhere near the same as hers. She'd taken such care to dress appropriately for a passionate session of lovemaking, and what had he said? "Don't worry, sweetheart, we'll talk."

"About what!" she shouted out in frustration, wracking her brain, but unable to come up with a single, satisfying answer.

Moments later, she leaped out of bed and went storming into the bathroom, intending to jump back into the shower and scrub off every ounce of the expensive French bath lotion she'd lavished on her body. When Paul came back he was going to find a woman who was in an entirely different frame of mind then the one he'd left—a howling, shrew of a woman dressed in sexless blue flannel instead of delicate black lace.

She had the offending teddy peeled down to the waist when she saw the phone. The receiver was half off the hook. Before concocting that ridiculous story about losing his keys, Paul had been speaking to somebody on the phone. But who? And what had been said that had caused him to rush out like that, not even caring if she believed his flimsy alibi or not?

"What the devil is going on here?" she questioned her image in the mirror, but the woman reflected there looked just as confused as she felt and just as lost for an answer.

Ten

———

It wasn't one or two, but almost three hours later that Tricia heard Paul's key being inserted into the lock. Curled up in a chair facing the door, she tucked the hem of her blue chenille bathrobe under her legs and waited. She tried to compose her features into a smooth mask, but with no success.

She was hurt and it showed. She was confused and it showed. She was spitting mad and that showed too.

Paul noted all three of those emotions in Tricia's expression as he let himself into their room, but his elation was so great that it couldn't be contained. With three swift strides, he covered the distance between them, bent down and scooped her up in his arms. Twirling her round and round, he proclaimed exuberantly, "I know how strange my behavior must have seemed to you tonight, but I couldn't explain anything to you until now. Sweetheart! I've got some really great news!"

With her arms locked around his chest and her face buried in his shoulder, Tricia's garbled response to that unexpected announcement was lost. Paul set her back down on her feet, but kept hold of her hand and started dragging her toward the upholstered couch placed beneath the window. After only one step, he was aware that she'd dug in her heels, unwilling to accompany him unless he offered a further explanation.

He turned back to face her and Tricia exclaimed in horror, "You're bleeding!"

Paul's smile faded slightly as he lifted his hand to his temple. At the slight show of blood on his fingers, he remarked sheepishly. "Damn, I thought that had stopped."

"What on earth have you done to yourself?" Tricia demanded shrilly, her imagination running with all sorts of wild possibilities.

Paul tossed off her concern with a self-dismissive shrug. "Don't worry about it, honey. It's just a little scratch I got falling down a couple of stairs. Now come over here and sit down. I've got so much to tell you."

The Cheshire cat grin he'd been sporting ever since he'd walked into the room returned to his face. "Tricia, the greatest thing in the world happened tonight."

Tricia allowed herself to be drawn across the room, mainly because she felt too disoriented to refuse. She'd gone over this scene in her mind countless times in the last three hours, but none of the scenarios she'd imagined had started out like this.

Besides the dark bruise over his left eye and the "little scratch" on his temple, Paul's clothing was a mess. His shirt was damp with sweat, his jacket was streaked with dust and his gray trousers had a jagged rip in the knee. He looked as if he'd just been mugged, yet sounded as if he'd enjoyed every minute of it.

"I don't know where to begin," he admitted once they were seated side by side on the couch. "You see, I—that is we, at the..." He broke off and tried again. "Tricia, I haven't been exactly..."

Tricia stared at him as his exuberant expression was slowly replaced by one of real anxiety. When it became clear to her that he was no longer quite so prepared to explain his admittedly odd behavior as he had been seconds before, she found her own voice. "You haven't been exactly what?"

Tricia became alarmed when Paul reached out and grabbed both of her hands as if he expected her to pull away from him the instant he opened his mouth. "I haven't been exactly honest with you."

Paul waited for her reaction to that damning admission. Tricia waited for him to explain what he meant by not being honest. When the waiting became interminable, they both started speaking at once, subsided abruptly back into silence, and then overlapped their apologies.

Paul shook his head. "Geez! I didn't act this awkward around you when I thought you were..."

Tricia's brows shot up. "When you thought I was *who*?"

Paul squeezed her hands, his tone urgent as he gazed deeply into her eyes. "Tricia, there's no easy way to tell you this so I might as well just come out with it and take my medicine. I know how you're going to feel, but I hope you'll be able to understand where I was coming from. I never meant to hurt you."

Barely stopping for his breath, he revised. "Well, at first your feelings about this weren't so much of an issue, but I didn't know you then like I do now, and I had a job to do, so what else could I have done? Anyway, I pray you'll find it in your heart to forgive me. I know what I did will seem pretty terrible to you, but I swear it's all over and behind us now and I hated every second of the time I had to deceive you."

In the entire time she had known Paul, which admittedly wasn't that long, Tricia had never seen him in such an agitated state. He was obviously trying to tell her something, but thus far, all she'd gleaned from his semicoherent ramblings was that he believed himself guilty of a major transgression against her that involved lying. Since she still didn't have any idea what he was talking about, she offered soothingly, "Of course I'll forgive you. Now will you please tell me what's so terrible? What's over and behind us?"

Before he could answer, she posed another question that had been eating away at her ever since he'd walked out of the room. "I know you spoke to somebody on the phone just before you left, Paul. Is that it? Is there someone in your past, another woman in your life that you haven't told me about? Did you go off and meet her tonight?"

If his dry chuckle and the words "In a weird kind of way, I suppose one could say that" were supposed to be reassuring, they were not. A sharp pain centered in her heart as she demanded, "I want to know if that's what *you're* saying?"

Paul shook his head, realizing that his ambiguous response had only added to her hurt and confusion.

While he'd been out clearing the way for their future together, she'd been busy building all sorts of problems between them that didn't exist. If he didn't want to make matters worse, he had to stop stalling and admit the truth. "Listen to me, Tricia. I've got something to tell you that you're going to find hard to believe and I want you to hear me out before you say anything, okay? Otherwise, I just might lose my nerve."

"Okay," Tricia agreed, since Paul's grasp on her hands was just short of painful.

As soon as he had her compliance, Paul took a deep breath and blurted out, "I left you alone tonight because I'm a special investigator for the FBI and I wanted to be in on the arrest of a notorious, female criminal who's evaded capture for years. At—"

"You're what!" Tricia yelped incredulously, certain she couldn't have heard right.

"Tricia, I told you what I had to say would be pretty hard for you to swallow, but you promised to listen until I was finished talking," Paul reminded her.

"But—"

"No buts!"

Her rebellious expression showed Paul that she wasn't going to hold to her promise unless he browbeat her into it. Since she was going to be angry anyway after he'd told her what he had to tell her, he didn't think he had that much to lose by swearing, "Dammit, Tricia! This is just as hard for me to explain as it is for you to accept. Is it asking too much for you to keep your mouth shut while I do?"

Lips clamped tightly together, Tricia pulled her hands out of Paul's grasp and folded her arms over her chest. If he wanted to continue with this craziness, she wouldn't stop him, but when she got her chance to speak, he was going to learn exactly how she felt about men who told whoppers to cover up their tomcat behavior. "So talk," she retorted indignantly.

Paul drew in a deep breath. "At the bureau, this woman I was telling you about is known as the 'Scarlet Lady' and she was hired by the Mangioni crime family to murder anyone who made trouble for their organization."

At the mention of that familiar name, Tricia's eyes flew to Paul's face and he nodded. "Your connection with Joe is one of the reasons you were suspected of being her. That's why I was assigned..."

"Me!" Tricia shrieked in shock. "A murderess! You actually thought I was...?" She shook her head as if to clear it, then beseeched the room at large. "What am I saying? Either I'm not hearing this right or this is some kind of a joke."

"There's nothing wrong with your hearing and I'm not joking," Paul interjected grimly.

Tricia stole another glance at his face and felt a sickening sensation in the pit of her stomach. Still unwilling to accept what he was saying, what she could see for herself in his expression, she deliberately turned her face away and asked, "Why are you doing this, Paul? What possible reason could you have for concocting a ridiculous story like this?"

"Look at me, Tricia, and you'll know that I'm telling you the truth," Paul ordered.

Reluctantly, Tricia did what he asked. "You're an FBI agent?"

"Yes."

"And you actually thought I was a murderess?"

"All the evidence pointed to that as a strong possibility."

"All what evidence?"

Tricia didn't have any difficulty keeping her mouth shut as Paul answered that question in mind-boggling detail. By the time he got done telling her the purpose of his undercover assignment at the Courteau farm, what he'd been expected to find out, and how his discoveries had increased the bureau's suspicions concerning her, she felt numb. When he proceeded to fill her in on the events that had finally cleared her of those suspicions, she couldn't have uttered a sound, even if her life had depended upon it.

In a matter-of-fact tone of voice, Paul was telling her that a woman she'd known quite well and had worked with for many years was a hit lady for the Mafia. Melinda Torrence, a fellow flight attendant at Trans-National, was a cold-blooded, contract killer known as the "Scarlet Lady." And if that wasn't enough of a shock for her, the fact that up until two hours ago, she herself had been suspected of being that killer, certainly was.

"Since the grand jury convenes tomorrow morning, we knew that one of you would make your move on our witness tonight. Of course, I had the edge on my fellow agents because I knew which one of you two it would be."

Unaware of Tricia's mounting hysteria, Paul laughed as he continued, "But to make Sam feel better, I followed his orders and vacated the premises so you could do the dirty deed if you felt so inclined. He raised holy hell when I left the door unguarded and came waltzing into the command post. I assured him that the hidden cameras would pick up your movements the instant you walked out into the hall, but a few seconds later, that assurance wasn't necessary.''

Paul searched Tricia's pale face. She was obviously shocked, but seemed more that willing to listen, so he went on, ''The screens were filled with pictures of Melinda Torrence heading down the hall toward our man's room. If you think that teddy you've got under your robe is sexy, you should've seen what she was wearing—a mink coat and nothing else. She looked like every man's sexual fantasy come to life.''

Tricia gave a weak laugh when she realized that it was expected of her, but it was almost her undoing. It took all of her strength to contain the insane giggles that threatened to follow behind that expression of amusement, and the effort showed.

''Are you all right?'' Paul inquired, his gaze narrowed on her pinched features. ''If you're not up to hearing the rest of this story, it can keep until morning. I know what a shock this must be for you. You think you know someone, but then you find out she's a . . .

''Never mind about her,'' Paul interrupted himself before he could utter the foul name that came to mind. ''Right now, all I'm concerned about is you. You're completely exhausted and hearing this has been too much for you, hasn't it? I should have waited until you'd had a decent night's sleep before dropping all this on you. It's just that I was so anxious to get this off my chest, I didn't think.''

When Tricia didn't say anything, just stared at him with the eyes of a wounded doe, Paul made what he felt was the wisest decision for them both. She wasn't up to hearing any more and he still had several hours of paperwork to do before he could return to her an entirely free man. He glanced at his watch. "Tell you what. I've got to go into the office and fill out my report before I can call it a night. Why don't you go to bed and get some rest? We can take up where we left off first thing tomorrow."

Tricia forced the words through her bloodless lips. "I . . . I am pretty tired."

She didn't have to fake the weakness in her limbs as Paul helped her to bed. If he considered exhaustion an acceptable excuse for her ashen complexion and the trembling in her legs, she was quite willing to go along with him. If reclining on the bed would hasten the time of his leaving, she was happy to recline. To ease the way for his departure, she allowed him to tuck her in beneath the blankets without screaming and she even suffered through the tender, farewell kiss he dropped on her lips without being sick.

"I'll be back before you know it," Paul promised as he headed for the door, unaware that Tricia took no comfort in the thought of his imminent return.

"Okay," she mumbled, turning her face into the pillows and keeping it there until she heard the door close behind him.

As soon as she felt it was safe, Tricia leaped out of bed and rushed to the closet, silently repeating the words, *You think you know someone but then you find out he's a . . .*

"Bastard!" she hissed, as she grabbed her suitcase and flung it onto the bed.

"Liar!" she snarled, the hot tears falling faster and faster as she whipped open the case and started throwing in her clothes.

"Imposter!" she declared, as she picked up the phone and dialed for a taxi to take her to the airport.

*   *   *

"For a woman who made life pretty damned miserable for us all these years, Ms. Torrence sure is doing a good job of smoothing the waters," Sam Mitchell announced as Paul entered his office. "She gave us a list of activities and names longer than my arm. Dates, times, payoffs. If we offer her enough of an incentive, she might even be willing to turn in the big man."

As he sank down in the chair before Sam's desk, Paul said, "Ironic, isn't it? The lady made a fair sum of money making hits and now she finds herself the target."

"Poetic justice is more like it," Sam decreed with a satisfied chuckle. "And you deserve most of the credit for bringing her in. We almost lost her in that stairwell."

Sam's commendation made Paul laugh. "Yes, indeed, if I hadn't tripped over my own feet and made all that noise falling down the stairs, we might never have flushed her out."

Sam couldn't keep a straight face. "Only an old hand at this game would have thought of using that old bumble-foot ploy. Those young college types we had with us tonight, would've never thought of it, let alone dare to risk it."

Paul went right along with the gag. "The new kids just don't have the experience to know when it's best to throw out the book and fly by the seat of your pants."

Sam had himself a good chuckle over that one, but sobered quickly when he saw Paul's face and realized that the time for joking around was about over. Leaning forward in his chair, Paul withdrew a folded sheet of paper from his breast pocket and placed it down on Sam's desk.

"Are you absolutely sure about this?" Sam inquired, eyeing the paper as if it were coated with some kind of noxious substance. "Don't you want a few more days to think it over? All kidding aside, you looked pretty good out there tonight, Lancelot."

"I've never been more certain about anything," Paul stated firmly.

Knowing he was grasping at straws, Sam proposed one last alternative. "You could go on the inactive duty roster for a while, but leave the way open for us to call you in for special assignments."

Paul smiled, but shook his head. "I've found my Camelot, Sam, so you can turn my white charger out to pasture. The lady of the castle needs this Lancelot at home and that's exactly where I want to be."

Unwilling acceptance shone in Sam Mitchell's eyes as he unfolded the piece of paper on his desk and read the brief statement. "According to the book, if I accept this letter of resignation, it puts you on thirty days' notice," he grumbled.

Paul lifted his arm to gaze at his watch. It was 8:00 a.m., almost seven hours since he'd left Tricia. She was bound to be waking up soon and he wanted to be there when she did. When she opened her eyes, he wanted the first sound she would hear to be him saying, "Patricia Courteau, I love you and I want you to marry me."

After giving the bureau over fifteen years of faithful service, Paul felt he deserved a little leeway in the regulations. "I read the same manual, Sam, but I could've sworn it said thirty seconds."

For a moment, Sam didn't say anything, but then he stood up and walked around the desk. Paul rose to meet him, accepting his outstretched hand. "Good luck, Lancelot. We're really going to miss you around here," Sam declared gruffly. "I hope that woman realizes how lucky she is."

"Once you meet her, you'll realize that I'm the lucky one, Sam," Paul stated simply. "We'll send you an invitation to the wedding."

"Are you sure she'll want me there?" Sam asked, as the two men left the office and began walking down the hall to the elevators. "After all, I'm the guy responsible for planting a phony hired hand in her house."

"I'm sure," Paul said firmly. "I haven't explained everything to her yet, but she's taken what I've told her so far like a real trooper. I can hardly believe it myself, and I know I don't deserve it, but that woman truly loves me, almost as much as I love her."

"Then you are a lucky man," Sam confirmed.

As Paul stepped into the elevator, it suddenly dawned on both men that they were about to close the door on a professional relationship that had existed for over a decade. Their eyes met in a visual bond. Neither of them was able to express in words the depth of feeling they had for one another, or the respect and admiration that had made them such a successful team.

Paul noted the glimmer in Sam's eyes as he felt the moisture collect in his own. Before pressing the button that would set him on course toward a new life, he said, "It was a great privilege and an honor to work with you, Chief Mitchell."

As the elevator doors slid shut, Sam proclaimed hoarsely, "Cut the baloney, Lancelot. I'll make sure you get your gold watch."

After a four-hour wait at O'Hare Airport, Tricia departed on a 7:00 a.m. flight to Dubuque. She arrived at nine-thirty and called her father to come pick her up. During the forty-minute drive to the farm, she told him why she'd flown home without Paul and as soon as they stepped into the house, he passed on the story to a stunned Leona and Aurie.

War had been waging ever since. At first, Tricia had been glad to sit back and listen as her parents expressed the same angry sentiments toward Paul that she had felt when he'd told her the truth about himself. Then, at some point during the conversation, she found herself defending him in her mind.

Though she had called him every name in the book since leaving Chicago, she didn't enjoy listening to the others doing the same. It was one thing for her to criticize the man she loved, but quite another to hear it coming from others, even if those others were her own parents.

As Tricia tried to analyze her ambivalent feelings, Leona declared," The man played us all for fools!"

"Hogwash!" Aurie exclaimed as she plunked down a fresh pot of coffee in the center of the kitchen table. "It wasn't Paul's intention to hurt anyone. The man had a job to do and he did it in the best way he knew how. Can't you see that?"

Yes, of course I can, Tricia acknowledged silently. *It's just that it came as such a shock.*

Leona wasn't willing to make the slightest concession. "Was it part of his job to sneak in here like a

thief in the night and steal my daughter's heart
away?'' she inquired heatedly, reaching for the coffee
pot and refilling the four empty cups at the table.
''Was it his job to convince her that he wanted to
marry her? I'm sorry, Mother Courteau, but I can't
excuse him for doing that.''

''Now, Leona,'' Aurie argued. ''We don't know
that his intentions were dishonorable.''

No, we don't, Tricia realized, beginning to regret her
rash decision to leave Paul before learning if getting
close to her had been part of his job or if he truly had
developed some deep personal feelings toward her. She
remembered the elated mood he'd been in just before
he'd made his shocking confession to her.

Her qualms increased as Aurie confirmed that it
could very well have been the latter. ''For all we know,
he might have meant everything he said and did while
he was here. Tricia left without giving the poor man a
chance to fully explain his side of the story.''

''He suspected our daughter of being a murderer!''
Mack refused to be persuaded. ''That's enough of an
explanation for me, and if he ever darkens this doorstep again, I'll let him know exactly how I feel about
that in no uncertain terms.''

''Well, I don't think we've any right to judge him so
harshly until we've heard all the facts,'' Aurie declared. ''Just as sure as I'm sittin' here, I know that
boy loves her.''

And that, Tricia realized was the crux of the matter. The outrage and betrayal she'd felt when Paul had
revealed the real reason he'd come to the farm had
overwhelmed her because he'd never given her those
three highly important little words. ''Paul never said

he loved me, Grannie," she murmured miserably. "Not even after we were supposedly engaged."

Aurie pursed her lips and shook her head. She looked at Tricia as if she should be ashamed of herself for even thinking something so ridiculous. "It pains me to hear you're still so blind where that man is concerned, so lacking in trust. Maybe Paul's the one who should be saying good riddance instead of it being the other way around."

"What a horrid thing to say!" Leona sputtered angrily as she saw the hurt and shock come over her daughter's face from Aurie's unexpected and uncalled for attack.

"Please, Mother," Mack began in a conciliatory tone, trying to ward off the inevitable explosion he knew was about to occur between his mother and his wife. "We realize that you like Paul and think we're being unfair to him, but that's no excuse for lashing out at Tricia."

"If she deserves it, it is," Aurie proclaimed bluntly. "And Tricia knows exactly what I'm talking about."

"Well, I never!" Leona exclaimed, preparing to launch a volley of words in defense of her cruelly maligned only child when that offspring intervened before the first shot could be fired.

"Grannie's right, Mom," Tricia stated with newfound yet unswerving conviction. "I have been wearing blinders where men are concerned ever since my engagement to Joe. Though I loved Joe and trusted him, he hurt me very badly, so badly that I've been afraid to give that love and trust again without demanding unconditional proof of its return. Grannie didn't say what she did to hurt me. She was just reminding me that I'm not that naive eighteen-year-old girl anymore, that I've grown up a great deal since then.''

"Of course you have. All of us realize that you're a mature woman now, but even a mature woman can be hurt by an unscrupulous, deceitful man," Leona said, still not wholly understanding what message Tricia was trying to convey to her, but anxious to reassure her daughter that she would always stand firmly on her side no matter what the circumstances.

"That's just it, Mom," Tricia said confidently. "Paul Lansing isn't unscrupulous or deceitful. He's strong and kind and generous and he loves me very, very much. He may not have said that in so many words, but I don't need the words to know that it's true. By his actions, he's given me all the proof any woman could ever want.''

"Tricia," Leona began, still perplexed. "I don't think I quite understand—''

"It would take too much time to explain everything right now, Mom, and I've got so much to do before Paul gets here," Tricia said as she stood up from her chair and marched across the room to pick up her suitcases.

"How do you know he's on his way here?" Mack inquired, just as taken aback by the sudden switch in his daughter's attitude as his wife.

"Where else would he go?" Tricia replied easily, a very serene, very happy smile on her face as she headed for the back stairs.

"Mother?" Mack turned to Aurie for an explanation as Tricia disappeared up the steps.

"I'll tell you all about it on the way to your place," Aurie announced, as she too stood up from the table and started out of the room. "I'll just go and pack my overnight bag and then we can leave."

"What the dickens is happening here, Mack?" Leona demanded of her husband who looked as if a light bulb had suddenly turned itself on in his head.

Mack reached across the table and patted his wife's hand. "Remember how it was when we first got married and were living here? Whenever we had a fight, Mother had the good sense to clear out so we could settle our differences in private. I think we owe our daughter a chance to do the same with the man she loves, don't you?"

A nostalgic smile came over Leona's face. "Oh my, yes, darling," she said, taking her husband's hand in her own and giving it an affectionate squeeze. "I most certainly think we do."

Eleven

On a warm night in early April, the city streets of Chicago were streaked with brown slush and intermittently lined with dwindling bands of dirt-encrusted ice. A never-ending flow of traffic, whizzing trains and bustling crowds provided a constant noise.

On a warm night in early April, the back roads of Iowa were clean and dry, though the ditches beside them brimmed with sparkling water. There was no traffic, no people, no noise, just the flickering lights from a distant farmhouse proclaiming the presence of man.

The fathomless heavens over that out-of-the-way house were lit by a brilliant spring shower of stars. A luminous, half-moon cast a soft, warm glow over the vast fields of moist, black earth on either side of the road. Each delicate leaf on the trees, each tender sprout pushing up from the ground, was touched by that gentle glow, as if the mighty hand of nature was reaching out to care for every individual plant in a loving way.

As Paul drove swiftly along the narrow, graveled road, the wheels of his pickup sending up a cloud of dust, he was struck by an acute sense of belonging. As he turned in by the metal mailbox, his headlights glanced off the groves of oak, maple and spruce along the long, slanted driveway, off the quaint wooden fences and the ancient windmill. And there, at the bottom of the hill, was the three-story white frame house with gingerbread trim and the big white barn.

After an exhausting ten-hour drive, he was finally home.

He parked the truck in front of the barn and got out, ignoring the stiffness in his muscles as he strode back up the driveway toward the house. As far as he was concerned, the discomfort he felt in his limbs was nothing compared to the pain he'd had to endure every second since he'd discovered that Tricia had walked out on him. When he'd returned to their hotel room and found her gone, he'd wanted to rush to the airport and board the very first plane taking off for Iowa. Then he'd remembered the truck.

No matter how anxious he was to set things straight with Tricia, he couldn't quite talk himself into leaving it behind. As hurt and angry as he'd been with her, he'd still felt obligated to return her belongings, even if those belongings were nothing but a bunch of empty wooden crates and the few unpopular items that she hadn't been able to sell at the craft fair.

Under the circumstances, Paul had every reason to believe she would welcome the return of her things far more graciously than she would the man who had

brought them. As far as Tricia was concerned, he was
a sneak and a liar and God knows what else. Even so,
he'd be damned if he'd let her throw away all the good
things they had going for them without putting up one
hell of a fight.

She was his woman and in a very few moments, she
was going to accept that fact, no matter how angry she
was with him. In the last two months, he'd filled himself up on her love and her warmth and her laughter.
He absolutely would not, could not, operate on empty
again!

Prepared to do battle, Paul marched up the sag-
ging back steps and onto the porch. He hung up his
jacket on a hook next to Tricia's blue parka and wiped
his shoes on the rubber-backed doormat so he
wouldn't track mud onto Aurie's clean floors. He
tugged the bottom of his blue V-necked sweater down
over the waistband of his gray cords, then took a deep
breath and pushed open the back door.

Though all the lights were on, the kitchen was unoccupied. A delicious, tangy odor was emanating from
the oven. A small pan of something was simmering on
the stove and a large wooden bowl filled with salad sat
upon the counter. The coffeemaker had just finished
brewing a fresh pot of coffee, but the table wasn't set
for a meal nor was there any sign of a cook.

It was going on 9:00 p.m. so the evening's chores
were done, yet Tricia wasn't seated in her customary
place at the kitchen table and Aurie's rocking chair
was unoccupied. Mack and Leona were nowhere in
sight. Where had they gone? Paul wondered gloomily. Had they seen the lights from his truck and immediately taken themselves off to another part of the

house so they wouldn't be there to greet him when he walked in the door?

"Tricia, Aurie," he called out loudly.

Silence.

The bitter taste of rejection rose like bile in his throat. In the back of his mind, he'd nursed the hope that Aurie would remain his ally even after Tricia had told her who he was and his purpose for coming to their farm. During the time it had taken him to drive the truck home, he had counted on Aurie to smooth the way for his return. He could see now that that hope had been in vain.

No matter how much affection Aurie held for him, blood was always thicker than water. He had hurt Tricia and, therefore, the Courteau family had closed ranks against him. In times of strife, a close-knit family was completely loyal to its own.

As much as he'd yearned to be a part of that family, he was still an outsider looking in at something he wanted but wasn't destined to have. Because of his professional loyalties, he'd destroyed any chance of fitting in. As a government agent, faithful to the service of his country, he could consider himself a success. But as a man, supposedly devoted in heart, body and spirit to the woman he loved, he had proved himself a dismal failure.

If Tricia couldn't or wouldn't believe that he loved her even if he'd come to her under false pretenses, what more could he do? Nothing, he realized. She either accepted him for who and what he was, or she didn't. By the looks of it, she didn't and neither did her parents or her grandmother.

As he yielded to the evidence before his eyes, all the fight went out of him. As much as the knowledge hurt,

Paul could see that there was no longer any place for him in the Courteau family. He had betrayed their trust and they couldn't forgive him for that, even knowing that he'd just been doing his job.

Now that he knew the way things stood, he didn't think he could stand having Tricia confirm it. It would be better for all concerned if he just turned around and left without causing a painful scene.

His hand was already on the doorknob when he heard Tricia's voice behind him.

"You made awfully good time."

"Yes." Anticipating what she was going to say next, Paul could barely force out that single word. Jaw clenched, he kept his back to her and waited.

Tricia willed him to turn round and look at her, see the love she felt for him shining in her eyes. She was dying to kiss him, to throw her arms around him and welcome him home, but then she heard an ominous hiss from the stove. Concerned for the welfare of the fabulous meal she'd just spent hours preparing, she dashed across the room in a flash and turned down the heat on the back burner.

Paul heard her mutter something under her breath, heard the clang of metal against metal and twirled round, just in case she was planning to throw something at him to get their confrontation underway. What he saw when he turned to face her made his mouth fall open.

He'd never seen her dressed like this before, in a long, black cashmere tube skirt that clung provocatively to the slender curves of her hips. It was slit almost up to the thigh, giving him an arousing glimpse of one sexy leg encased in black-textured hose. Above the tight skirt, she wore a war-paint red, silk camisole

that vividly outlined her high, full breasts. Her shimmering black hair was swept up off her nape in an el-
egant French twist that exposed the graceful lines of
her throat and the creamy perfection of her neck and
shoulders.

Other than the tiny diamond studs at her ears, she
wore no other jewelry and as far as Paul was concerned she didn't need any other adornment. She was
so breathtakingly beautiful, all he could do was slump
back against the door and stare at her.

Paul was so caught up in his visual study, he barely
heard Tricia as she said, "I thought it would be more
relaxing for you after your long drive if we ate dinner
in the living room. I set up a table in front of the fireplace. Why don't you go on in, pour yourself some
Chianti and get comfortable while I finish up in here.

"I hope like heck he likes Italian," she muttered
worriedly to herself as she bent down to remove a cas-
serole dish from the oven. Once assured that the
chicken tetrazzini was baked to perfection, she sprin-
kled Parmesan cheese over the top, then placed the
dish on a heavy silver tray next to the bowl of Caesar
salad. She placed two salad bowls and the bun warmer
in the last empty spaces between dishes, gave the
kitchen counter a final glance to make sure she hadn't
forgotten anything, then picked up the heavy tray.

She had only taken a step when she realized that
Paul hadn't moved a muscle since she'd last spoken to
him. Her face fell as she looked at him. His features
looked as if they'd been cut out of iron, his eyes as
hard and cold as steel. It was going to take much more
than a sexy outfit and a fancy home-cooked meal to
appease him. "I guess you're still pretty mad at me,
aren't you?" she inquired tentatively.

Her question seemed to startle him out of some sort of trance. "Huh?"

Tricia sighed. The poor man was obviously dead on his feet and that, too, was all her fault. Even so, she urged pleadingly, "Oh, Paul, can't we wait until after we've eaten to get into it? You look so tired."

Paul cleared his throat and declared gruffly, "No, I'm not tired at all."

Tricia tried another tack. "But you've got to be hungry and I wanted this meal to be perfect. It won't taste any good at all if we don't eat it while it's hot."

Paul glanced at the tray she was carrying, then back at her face. What she was saying was finally starting to sink in. She wasn't planning to cast him out, she was welcoming him home! As he considered that amazing turn in events, relief surged through him like a healing balm and the painful knots that wrenched his insides slowly began to unravel.

The expression on Paul's face was completely new to Tricia and she didn't quite know how to take it. His gray eyes were so intent on her features, it felt as if he were trying to see inside her very soul. Yet, when he spoke, his voice sounded casual, almost disinterested. "Won't Aurie or your folks be joining us?"

Tricia swallowed hard. She couldn't get a grip on him in this strange mood. He didn't look that angry, but she could feel the tension radiating from him like a physical force. She didn't know whether or not it was wise to tell him that they had the whole house to themselves. Unfortunately, beneath his unrelenting gaze, she didn't dare lie. "Mom and Dad left for home this afternoon. Grannie . . . well, she thought it might be best if she went with them."

"I see," Paul stated evenly, but there was nothing calm in his expression as he pushed his shoulders away from the door and took a step toward her. "Then you and I are all alone here."

Tricia moistened her lips nervously as she noted the smoldering light in his gray eyes and his brief ravening smile. "They thought we might like some privacy."

"They thought right," Paul stated in a deep and sensual tone that sent a ripple of excitement through her.

Suddenly, Tricia was aware of him in a way she'd never been before. For the first time since she'd found out who he really was and how he'd made his living, she saw him as an unpredictable, highly trained and powerfully dangerous man. Paul Lansing wasn't some happy-go-lucky, aimless drifter, searching for something he could never seem to find. He was a straightforward and determined man who knew exactly what he wanted and he wasn't going to let anything stand in the way of his getting it.

Tricia gulped on the certain knowledge that what he wanted right now was her. Realizing that she commanded the desire of such a man was an awesome thought. She, Patricia Courteau, a plain, ordinary, everyday kind of woman from a backwater town in Iowa had a real, honest-to-goodness G-man in love with her. It truly boggled the mind.

"Something disturbing you, Tricia?" Paul inquired, wanting to laugh as he noted the agitation in her breathing. "All of a sudden, you look as if you're a bit frightened. Now why is that, do you suppose?"

"Of course I'm not frightened."

But she was, Paul realized, and after all the needless pain and suffering he'd endured on her account, he couldn't resist baiting her a little. "Perhaps you were wondering what a man like me does with a woman who's just put him through ten hours of hell."

Watching his approach, Tricia's eyes went very wide. "He lets her fix him a really scrumptious meal to make amends?"

Paul came to a stop in front of her. "The way I feel right now, I plan to make a meal of something all right."

"Good." Tricia thrust out the serving tray to him. "Then if you wouldn't mind taking this into the living room for me, we can start eating. I...um...think I forgot something in the refrigerator."

Never releasing her eyes from his gaze, Paul accepted the tray and placed it down on the kitchen table. "As hungry as I am," he continued as if she hadn't spoken, his hands closing around her upper arms, "dinner will just have to wait until I get answers to a few questions."

"What questions?" Tricia whispered tremulously just before she was hauled against him and his mouth came down hard onto hers.

Do you still love me? his hungry lips inquired as they drank the sweetness from her mouth.

Yes, oh yes, hers replied, as her arms lifted to circle his neck and her body melded joyously to his.

Do you know now that I love you too? he asked as a shudder of unceasing desire ripped through him and his muscles trembled from the effort of restraint.

Tricia heard his silent question in her heart, sensed his restraint with her body and felt his urgency through her skin. As much as she wanted to stay right where she was, she had an equally desperate need to see his face when he verbally acknowledged the truth. Arching her back, she pulled her mouth away from his.

"I love you with all of my heart," he confirmed, smiling down at her smile. A moment later, his eyes narrowed on something he saw in her face. "You knew that before I said it, didn't you? You knew it even before I walked in that door tonight."

Tricia nodded.

He gave her a little shake, unable to hide his frustration. "Then why, why did you run out on me like that, Tricia? Didn't you realize what that would do to me? I thought I had lost you, that when you learned the truth about me, your love turned to hate."

Tricia shook her head. "I was angry with you for using me like that, but I couldn't hate you even if I tried." Her expression grew rueful as she admitted, "And I tried so hard, I almost had myself convinced."

"What happened to unconvince you?"

"After mulling things over for a while I decided that you're not the kind of man who would lure a murder suspect into bed just to find out if she's got homicidal tendencies."

"Thanks," Paul retorted, but then the meaning behind her words got through to him and his features twisted into a thunderous scowl. "You actually thought that was why I made love to you?" he demanded. "After all we've shared together, how in hell could you have thought that?"

"Well, I wasn't thinking too clearly at the time," Tricia acknowledged. "If you recall, I'd just found out that everything about you was a lie from the very first moment we met."

"I never lied about my reasons for wanting you," Paul bit out tersely, greatly offended. "And you know damned well they didn't have anything to do with your being a murder suspect."

"I was twenty thousand feet in the air before I reached that same conclusion," Tricia agreed. "I played back every word you'd ever spoken to me and realized that you hadn't seduced me as part of your investigation, but out of pure and simple lust."

"What!" Paul was even more outraged than he had been before.

Trying not to wince beneath the hard fingers digging into her arms, Tricia continued on blithely, "Well, you have to admit that you never told me you loved me."

"The hell I didn't!" Paul blustered furiously, then remembered that before tonight, he'd never said the words out loud. Even so, he accused, "Lady, if you didn't realize that I've loved you ever since I first set eyes on you, then you've got pretty lousy perception."

Tricia slid her arms around his waist and rested her head against his warm shoulder. "So I was told."

"By whom?" Paul wanted to know, though the feel of Tricia's soft breasts against his chest and her caressing hands on his back were making it awfully hard to concentrate.

"Grannie," she confirmed, as she pulled up his sweater and began running her fingertips up and down his taut spine. "She helped me to remember that a man's actions are the best proof of his feelings."

Gratified by his response, her fingers slid back around to the front and began to work on the front fastening of his slacks. "Going by yours, the only conclusion I could reach was that you're madly, passionately in love with me and have been for quite some time."

Paul sucked in his breath as the button on his slacks gave way beneath her roaming fingers. He didn't know whether to be pleased by her assessment of his recent behavior or not. This woman had given his ego a very thorough going-over and he wasn't sure he should let her maintain such a cocksure attitude where his greatest vulnerability was concerned.

On the other hand, he didn't have the strength to deny what her caresses were doing to him. "What about your behavior?" he challenged thickly, as he slid the thin straps of her camisole down her arms. Cupping her bared breasts in his palms, he stroked her with his thumbs and she gasped for breath. When he lowered his head and kissed her tautened nipples, she moaned in pleasure. "Isn't this proof that you're just as madly and passionately in love with me?"

"You bet your sweet life it is," Tricia vowed fervently. "I need you so much, Paul."

With a half relieved, half exultant laugh, Paul whisked her up off of her feet and into his arms. "Then I'm taking you upstairs to bed so I can show you that the feeling's entirely mutual."

"Sounds good to me," Tricia giggled as Paul strode toward the back stairs.

"I hope getting married sounds just as good," Paul retorted, increasing his speed as they neared the second floor landing. "Because first thing tomorrow morning we're going to apply for a license."

"We'll have to elope if we don't want my mother and Grannie to arrange the biggest wedding Jackson County has ever seen."

Paul stopped dead in his tracks. "Do you want a big church wedding, Tricia? If you've got your heart set on that, we can wait."

"I've got my heart set on marrying you as soon as possible," Tricia replied firmly. "And I don't want to wait a single second longer than we have to. Besides, by tomorrow morning, I plan to be so utterly, hopelessly compromised you'll be lucky if my father isn't waiting downstairs with a shotgun just to make sure that you do the right thing."

"I'm surprised he wasn't waiting for me with one when I drove in tonight," Paul admitted as he lowered her down on his bed.

"He wouldn't dare shoot the man I love full of holes," Tricia quipped, then saw that Paul had been serious. "Grannie never doubted you, Paul, and my folks stopped doubting as soon as I told them that you never meant to hurt or mislead any of us, but were only doing your job. Of course, it might be wise if you told them that not once in the entire time you were here did you ever think me guilty of being a hit lady for the Mafia."

Tricia's brows shot up as she noted the telltale flush on Paul's face. "Don't tell me that you did?"

Paul pulled his sweater up over his head as he mumbled, "Maybe just once." Before pulling it all the way off, he waited to hear her reaction. When it came in the form of loud, uninhibited laughter, he whisked the sweater off the rest of the way. "It's not that funny. If you recall, you were carrying a gun the night I first met you and the next day you injected all those poor little piglets with the same kind of poison used by the 'Scarlet Lady.'"

"So that's why you were so green around the gills that day," Tricia hooted, holding her stomach to contain her laughter. "No wonder I scared you to death when I threw myself at you on the way into town."

"I was *not* scared."

"Yes, you were," Tricia insisted, brown eyes sparkling with delight as she warmed to the ridiculous notion. "You were terrified that I'd planned to ensnare you with my wicked womanly wiles."

In the next second, Tricia found herself pinned to the mattress by a very warm, marvelously naked male body. "And your evil plan worked, didn't it?" Paul accused, as he began to pull her skirt down over her hips. "Now I'm yours forever."

"Hopelessly locked in my web," Tricia boasted, moving swiftly to assist him in his efforts to remove her clothes.

"Hopelessly," Paul conceded thickly as his eyes worshiped the beautiful sight laid out before him.

Tricia gazed back at the beautiful man leaning over her, her own eyes expressing their fair share of awe. Lifting her arms to him, she whispered softly, lovingly, "Welcome home, my darling. Welcome home."

AT LAST YOU CAN FIND
TRUE ROMANCE ON TELEVISION!

PRESENTING THE SHOWTIME●

Romance Movie

─────── S E R I E S ───────

Full-scale romance movies, taken from your favorite
Romance novels. Beautifully photographed on
location, it's romance the way you've always
dreamed. Exclusively on Showtime cable TV!

ROMANCE ON SHOWTIME
COMING ATTRACTIONS:

DREAMS LOST, DREAMS FOUND: Based on the
novel by Pamela Wallace, starring Kathleen Quinlan.

ONLY ON SHOWTIME

This summer, you'll also see **Exclusive Movies** such
as:
- **HEARTBURN** starring Meryl Streep,
  Jack Nicholson
- **RUTHLESS PEOPLE** starring Bette Midler
- **EXTREMITIES** starring Farrah Fawcett
- **KISS OF THE SPIDER WOMAN** starring
  William Hurt

ROMANCE ON SHOWTIME—THE ONLY
PLACE ON TV TO FIND TRUE ROMANCE!

SHOWTIME.●

CALL YOUR CABLE COMPANY TODAY TO ORDER SHOWTIME

SMV-B-1